Carl Weber Presents:
Ride or Die Chick 2

Carl Weber Presents:
Ride or Die Chick 2

by

J.M. Benjamin

www.urbanbooks.net

Urban Books, LLC
97 N18th Street
Wyandanch, NY 11798

Carl Weber Presents: Ride or Die Chick 2

ISBN 13: 978-1-62286-930-5
ISBN 10: 1-62286-930-3

First Mass Market Printing November 2015
First Trade Paperback Printing October 2014
Printed in the United States of America

10 9 8 7 6 5 4 3 2 1

*This is a work of fiction. Any references or similarities
to actual events, real people, living, or dead, or to real
locales are intended to give the novel a sense of reality.
Any similarity in other names, characters, places, and
incidents is entirely coincidental.*

Distributed by Kensington Publishing Corp.
Submit Orders to:
Customer Service
400 Hahn Road
Westminster, MD 21157-4627
Phone: 1-800-733-3000
Fax: 1-800-659-2436

This book is dedicated to all the women who stand by the men they love.

Acknowledgments

Eternal thanks to the Most High for allowing me the strength to keep moving forward and never looking backwards. Without Your guidance I would be lost.

Thanks to my family and few friends who have been and continue to be a major asset and supporter in all that I do. I wish you all nothing but the best.

Thanks to all of my readers old and new: Without you I would not have a voice in this game.

Much love to the many incarcerated men and women around the world who may have or may not have read a J.M. Benjamin book. My story behind the stories I write is your story. Continue to believe there are better days ahead, because there really is life after incarceration.

Peace
J.M. Benjamin

Prologue

Her vision was blurry as she opened her eyes. She had been under heavy observation for the past four days, expected not to survive. It had been a crucial and life-threatening four days, but being the strong individual she was, she had survived, although she felt a little weak. She had no clue as to where she was, not even aware that she was unconscious for a period of time. Upon gaining some of her sight, she began trying to focus on where it was she was actually at. She attempted to wipe her heavy eyelids, feeling the coal on them that made it difficult to clear her vision, but came up with a short hand, now realizing she had been handcuffed to something.

With her free hand, she wiped her eyes and as her vision became clearer, she noticed she had been handcuffed to a hospital bed. But that was not all. She had a tube stuck in her chained-up arm, which ran from a machine and saw another one running from a machine up under her hospital gown. For the life of her, she couldn't figure out how she wound up in a hospital cuffed to a bed and why. Her memory was a blur, and she had no recollection of what had taken place days ago. She began moving, only to find out her whole entire body was sore. But why? She had no clue.

She continued looking around, searching for clues that would give her some indication how she was in the predicament she was in. As she looked to her left she spotted a newspaper on the hospital nightstand next to the bed. She painfully reached over and grabbed the paper. The date read October 28, 2007, and she couldn't determine whether the newspaper was actually that day's or yesterday's, because she had no knowledge as to what day it really was. The front page had a heading that stuck out to her, but she didn't know why. It read in big, bold letters: THE BONNIE AND CLYDE OF THE NEW MILLENNIUM. Up under the heading was a picture of a black CLS. Even before she began reading the article, the car triggered something inside her as images of it began to fill her mind, causing her to remember some things. Within the first four lines tears began to roll down her face. Reading her soul mate's name caused Teflon to regain all of her senses and have her thoughts restored. Everything all made sense now. October 28 was the day they decided to rob the bank. The heading *Bonnie and Clyde of the new millennium* referred to her and Treacherous. The Mercedes was the car she and Treacherous had jacked and murdered the two young dealers for to use on the bank job. She had taken a shot to the side as they were coming out of the bank, and Treacherous had taken the police on the high-speed chase in attempts to get her to the hospital, which was all she could remember. As she continued to read, the rest was answered for her in black-and-white; how Treacherous had gone all out right there on the Virginia Beach exit while she lay there unconscious.

Teflon's tears flowed harder as she envisioned the scene. She knew there was only one thing that no one else could know besides her, which would make Treacherous take the route he took. The only thing that would have made her take the same route had the situation been different and she was in his shoes: if one thought the other was dead. How could he have thought she was dead? she wondered. Was her pulse or heartbeat that low that it went undetected? Teflon wanted to know the answers to those questions, because they were the answers that caused her to lose her other half—or her better half, as Treacherous would say. She smiled at the thought. She remembered when Treacherous had first told her about the bank and how he had said that after that day every dude and chick would be comparing themselves to Treacherous and Teflon. He had said they were like Bonnie and Clyde and Romeo and Juliet all wrapped up in one, but harder, and everything he said was coming to pass. Teflon herself had viewed their love for each other as a Romeo-and-Juliet relationship because they too were young and in love, and just as Romeo took his own life, assuming Juliet had been dead, Treacherous had basically done the same. And just as Juliet woke, only to find out that Romeo was dead, so did Teflon. She began beating herself up, knowing had she not been unconscious she and Treacherous would have gone out together in a blaze of glory. She began ripping the tubes from up out of her in an attempt to find a way to take her own life, just as Juliet did, so she could meet up with her soul mate again.

While in the process of doing all of this, the doctor walked in, catching Teflon in the act and rushed over to her.

"Ms. Jackson!" the doctor yelled, grabbing her free hand.

"Calm down. You're all right. You and the baby are going to be fine, just take it easy."

Up until his last statement Teflon continued to resist the doctor's attempts to restrain her, but hearing what he just said registered enough to get her to instantly stop what she was trying to do.

"What did you just say?" she asked the doctor, making sure she had heard him correctly, as she cleared her throat.

"I said to take it easy, you and the baby are going to be fine," he repeated. Right then Teflon noticed the officer, who she assumed stood guard by her room door, stick his head inside.

"Is everything all right, doc?" the white young-looking officer asked, hearing all the commotion from the hallway.

"Yes, everything is fine," the doctor replied, not wanting to cause a scene or get the pretty young girl in any more trouble than she was already in.

By now, Teflon had calmed down completely after getting the doctor's confirmation on his last statement.

"That's better," expressed the doctor as he started reattaching the tubes that Teflon had snatched out of her.

He assumed she had awakened and wigged out at the sight of everything, which he thought to be normal in her case, after experiencing such a traumatic event days ago. He himself couldn't

believe how such a beautiful-looking woman
could be mixed up in such an ugly ordeal and
have dealings with a man of the young man's
caliber that he had read about in the newspaper
and seen plastered all over the news, but had
he known the extent of their bond and relationship, he would not have been so quick to doubt
Teflon's ruthlessness. He had left the newspaper
on the nightstand next to her bed for whenever
she awoke, figuring she would want to know the
outcome of the serious situation she had just
survived, which he felt she was probably forced
into. How could she have gone along with such
a plan on her own free will, as innocent as she
appeared to look? But because he had grown up
with practically a silver spoon in his mouth and
was naive as green, artificial grass when it came
to the streets, he could only a judge a book by its
cover without knowing the truth and depths of
the contents inside.

"It's good to see you awake. We thought we
were going to lose you, but you're a strong young
woman."

Teflon watched him as his hand slid under the
hospital blanket with the intent of reconnecting
the tube that was once stuck in her side. She
felt his hand brush up against her bare hips and
flinched. No other man had touched her body

in over twelve years besides Treacherous, and the thought of the doctor's foreign hand on her brought chills through her body.

"I got it," she said, moving the doctor's hand.

"Oh, I'm sorry," said the doctor, thinking he had hurt her. "Are you sore?"

"Yeah, a little."

"All right. I'll see to it that you get something to help with the pain and for infections as well. You took a nasty hit. It was iffy in the operating room."

"How long was I unconscious?" Teflon asked.

"Four days."

"Damn. What about the baby? How long have I been pregnant?" she asked.

"You mean you didn't know?" the doctor asked, surprised.

"If I did, I wouldn't have asked," replied Teflon, her attitude becoming agitated.

The doctor caught the hostility mixed with sarcasm and blamed it on Teflon's condition.

"You're five weeks pregnant."

Teflon thought back to the last time she and Treacherous had made love and began to smile at the thought, as tears streamed down her face once again. Their last encounter was the time she had awoke, only to find Treacherous masturbating with one hand while he had his other one between her thighs. She remembered all too well and realized that had she not replaced his hand with her love box that day, she would not have a part of him growing inside of her. Adding this new piece to the equation caused Teflon to rethink her plans. There was nothing else she wanted more in life than to join Treacherous wherever he was, whether it be heaven or hell, but because of the five-week-old life that dwelled inside of her, her plans to meet up with her better half would have to be delayed and their reunion would have to be put on hold; at least for another seven months.

Chapter 1

"All rise for the Honorable Judge William H. Braswell of the District of Virginia."

Teflon sighed in frustration as she struggled to lift herself up out of the wooden courtroom chair. She was sick and tired of being lugged back and forth to court month after month for something she already knew the final outcome of. She felt it had been a long and drawn-out case. When she first laid eyes on the jurors who would determine her fate, there was no doubt in her mind what type of verdict would be handed down. Seeing them over to her far right now, and the way they stared and murmured among themselves, only confirmed Teflon's thoughts. The only reason she had actually taken her case to trial was because she knew it was what Treacherous would have wanted her to do. "We fighters, babe, we go hard or go home," he would always say to her, Teflon recalled. She fought to suppress her emotions at the thought of her other half as a sharp pain jolted through the small of her back. Between the spasms she had been having since the gunshot wound she was recovering from and the nine-month-old life growing inside of her, her movement was turtle-like and painful. As tough as she was, she was no match for the battle she had been going through with the life inside of her. Noticing her facial expressions, her attorney made an attempt to aid her. It was apparent to him that she was in pain, but he was stopped in his tracks by her sudden expression that spoke volumes, making it perfectly clear to him that his services were not welcomed nor needed. After representing her for the last eight months, he had grown accustomed to her nonchalant and cold demeanor, so he was not at all surprised that she had declined his help. Teflon stood in front of the table with her hair pulled back in a ponytail, sporting her gray county sweat suit and county-issued tennis shoes. She used the table to brace herself as the judge entered the courtroom. The additional twenty-one pounds she put on between the baby and jail made it that much more difficult for her to stand. The weight was uncomfortable for her and she couldn't wait to shed both it and the baby and get back to her normal size of nine-ten.

"Please be seated," the judge instructed

"Umph," Teflon grunted as another spasm shot through her lower back.

"This is the trial of *the United States of America versus Teflon Jackson*. Counsels, state your names for the record."

"Your Honor, Mark Stanford of the public defender's office of Norfolk for the defense," announced Teflon's attorney

"Christopher Malloy, district attorney of Norfolk for the prosecution, Your Honor."

"If I'm correct, today is the final day of this trial," the judge stated, skimming through the paperwork before him. "Counsels will deliver their closing arguments and remarks and the jury will render a verdict based on the information and evidence that has been presented to them throughout this trial. Counsel, are you ready to proceed?"

"Yes, Your honor, " both counsels replied.

"Mr. Stanford."

This was the moment of the truth, thought Mark Stanford. He took one look back at Teflon and slightly shook his head in disbelief as he sighed to himself. In exchange, Teflon stared him right in the eyes, unfazed by his sympathetic eyes. He couldn't believe how hard-core Teflon was and had been throughout the entire

time of his representation. In his thirteen years
of practice as a public defender, he had never
encountered a client more difficult and rebel-
lious than Teflon Jackson. In the eight months
he had been her lawyer, from day one she was
uncooperative. It had been like pulling teeth
trying to get her to open up in order to assist
him in trying to soften the blow of what he knew
was her inevitable fate, according to what he had
read and discovered about the case. There were
a few angles and approaches he would have liked
to have taken for her defense, but Teflon refused
to talk with him after stating she wanted to go
to trial. She wouldn't budge even when he tried
to appeal to her maternal side; still, she rejected
the notion of helping him help her, so his only
defense was based on the lack of evidence they
actually had against her. Attorney Stanford sympathized with the pregnant young woman, but
due to his heavy workload and promising cases
of clients who were willing to help themselves as
well as the government in exchange for leniency,
he was all too happy to be bringing this particular case to a close. Mark Stanford took a sip of
the ice water that sat before him and cleared
his throat. "Members of the jury," he started
as he walked from behind the court table
and adjusted his tricolor necktie. "In the past

few months you have heard allegations from the prosecution against my client that make her out to look like not only this modern-day Bonnie from Bonnie and Clyde, but also this stone-cold killer. As you know, Ms. Jackson is being charged with multiple counts of conspiracy to commit armed robbery in the first degree and conspiracy to commit murder in the first." He let the accusations of the charges linger before he continued. "But what she is being accused of and charged with is not the case here today. No." He paused.

"The case here is what evidence has been presented to substantiate these allegations against my client." He paused again, then pivoted.

"The prosecution would like you to be convinced that my client, Ms. Teflon Jackson, conspired to commit armed robbery, but yet he failed to produce any surveillance video clearly showing my client's direct involvement in the allegation. Nor was he able to produce a witness from inside the bank who could testify to the fact of whether or not my client was held against her own free will by the deceased Mr. Treacherous Freeman."

His words and the mentioning of Treacherous's name instantly gained her attention and rubbed Teflon the wrong way. She had no idea or

clue as to her attorney's closing arguments and
really didn't care up until the time he had just
tried to portray her as the victim and her other
half as the villain. She was tempted to jump up
and set the record straight, but Treacherous's
words danced in her head as if he were right
beside her. "Using emotions over intellect is
never justifiable," she heard him repeating.

Why the fuck you leave me like this? Teflon
questioned in her mind, staring up to the ceiling
as if Treacherous were up there looking down at
her. She grabbed a napkin off the table to wipe
her left nostril. It began to run. She sat up and
became attentive as her lawyer continued. "The
prosecution states that my client is guilty of
conspiracy to commit *murder*," attorney Stanford said with emphasis, turning to face Teflon
and pointing in her direction. He could tell she
was not too pleased by the comment he had
made about her deceased boyfriend. He knew
he would be treading on thin ice with her by
painting the picture he just had, but it was the
only way he felt he could help spare her life. He
was fully aware of the bond the couple shared.
He had found out firsthand a few months back,
when he had made the fatal mistake of merely
referring to Treacherous as *this guy* and making
mention of him being deceased. At forty-three

years old, standing at five feet ten, tipping the scales at 215 pounds, he had never been so afraid of someone who he outweighed, and he'd felt outmatched in his life that day. And to top it off, it had been a woman who had instilled this fear within him. It wasn't anything she had done—but what she had said and how she had said it—which sent chills throughout Mark Stanford's entire body. He couldn't help but replay the words that invaded his sleep many nights: "If you ever speak of my deceased loved one in vain in my presence ever again you're gonna meet him."

The calm manner in which she spoke convinced him that she meant every word of it. His first instinct was to report the incident and abandon the case, but his curiousness overpowered his decision. He wanted to see how this particular case unfolded and wanted to be the one who played a part in its unfolding.

"But yet, none of the murder weapons retrieved from the crime scene possessed my client's fingerprints."

His words caused Teflon to peer over toward the jurors' direction. She noticed a few puzzled and quizzical expressions on a few of their faces. She knew that a key element of her case would stir up some, if not a great deal, of confusion

among them. That was something she herself
was confused about initially, knowing her involvement like she knew the back of her own
hand. As she played the tapes back to the event,
there was no doubt in her mind that she had hit
at least one of the officers when they came out of
Bank of America, before she herself took one in
the side. The only explanation possible she could
come up with was that Treacherous had wiped
her prints off the gun she used, but why? That
was something she would not get the answer
to until the two of them met up in the future,
she reasoned. Teflon listened as her attorney
continued.

"Yes, my client is guilty. But not guilty of the
charges she sits here with child being accused
of." Attorney Stanford paused for a second time
to let the statement about Teflon being with
child marinate. "The only thing my client is
guilty of here today is loving a man too much
and too hard," he said. He really wanted to say,
"Loving the wrong man," but he didn't want to
go overboard with offending his client. Teflon's
threat months ago sat at the forefront of
his mind and he thought better of it. "And that,
ladies and gentlemen, is not why my client is on
trial here today. I hope you take all that I've said
into account when making your ruling."

Attorney Stanford ended with a bow and walked back around the table where Teflon sat. The two exchanged quick glances. Teflon gave her attorney no indication that she approved of his argument and he wasn't looking for one. After all, it was his job. District Attorney Christopher Malloy skimmed through his notes one last time before he stood. He then looked over at Teflon, who felt his eyes on her.

"What the fuck you lookin' at?" she mumbled under her breath just enough for him to hear and read her lips. The DA smiled and pushed his glasses up on his face. He had no sympathy whatsoever for the female criminal who sat across from him. According to the evidence, there was no doubt in his mind or heart that Teflon Jackson deserved all that she would receive and then some after a verdict was handed down. Despite what he was able to produce to build a strong case against her, he was confident the jury would render the right decision and continue to keep the female menace to society off the streets. It was DA Malloy's intent to push for the maximum penalties, providing the verdict was what he believed it would be. "Ladies and gentlemen of the jury. Despite what counsel says the prosecution failed to produce, there has been evidence presented to you that clearly shows that the accused is in fact guilty of the charges she stands trial for. Evidence showed that Ms. Teflon Jackson and Mr. Treacherous Freeman exited the Norfolk, Virginia branch of Bank of America with weapons and were involved in a gun battle with police. Evidence clearly showed that there was a high-speed pursuit for Ms. Jackson and the deceased, endangering the welfare of other pedestrians and law enforcement. Evidence showed that the vehicle used as the getaway car was in fact the same car that was carjacked at a local McDonald's, resulting in two murders. Evidence also shows that during this crime spree, six state police officers and four federal agents were killed in the line of duty, while five others were wounded. I'm not standing before you trying to convince you to speculate or even try to figure out what I didn't or why I didn't present the evidence counsel said I failed to produce. All I ask is that you look at the evidence that was presented to you by the courts and based on that and that alone render the decision that you feel fits. Thank you," DA Malloy clasped his hands together and ended with a slight bow to the jury. He then returned to the table opposite of Teflon and her attorney. She rolled her eyes at the district attorney. When he sat down, he looked over at Teflon again, who now had a gun of her own plastered across her face. He had no way of knowing that Teflon was visualizing Treacherous pistol-whipping him with the butt of his gun while she stood there and watched.

"Members of the jury. You have heard both arguments in the case of *the United States of America versus Teflon Jackson*. It is your duty, after hearing both parties and based on the evidence presented before you, that beyond a reasonable doubt a decision is made. It's now ten forty-five a.m. The court will recess for an hour while the jury returns to chambers. Bailiff, please escort the jury back to chambers," the judge ordered with his gavel. Hearing that, the two marshals sitting two rows behind Teflon and her attorney stood and approached the front of the courtroom. "Ms. Jackson, please stand and turn around," the female marshal requested with handcuffs in hand. Teflon exhaled and complied, and the cuffs were then placed around her wrists. "Too tight?" the marshal asked. Teflon answered with a nod. "I'll be back there to see you shortly," her attorney announced as Teflon was escorted through the court and to the federal holding cell. She didn't bother to acknowledge that she had heard his words. Attorney Stanford and the male federal marshal exchanged glances. In their line of work they were all too used to detainees acting the way Teflon was. "Okay, let me get these cuffs off you," the federal marshal said. "I'll be back to check on you periodically and I'll see if I can get you a pillow or blanket," the female marshal added as she locked Teflon in the bullpen. Being a mother herself, she empathized with Teflon. She recognized labor symptoms when she saw them. She knew Teflon would deliver her child any day now. The female marshal shook her head in sadness at Teflon's present condition and situation as she and her parties exited the holding quarters. Teflon's hold on the bullpen's bench slowly made her way to the floor. The bench was too small and uncomfortable for her, so she chose the floor instead, using the edge of the bench for support. In just under an hour she would receive closure on this chapter of her life. Despite her attorney's best attempt to defend her, Teflon knew she would not be walking up out of her situation scot-free—not now, not later, or if at all. And she had come to terms with herself with that. And when she felt she could no longer take it, she'd meet up with Treacherous again. She lifted up her sweatshirt and white T underneath and began rubbing her stomach in a circular motion as images of her last moments with her other half flashed through her mind.

"Treach," yelled Teflon as she pointed her .380 and 9 mm butler in the direction of the police and began squeezing the triggers. "Babe, get in!" Treacherous yelled over to Teflon, attempting to cover her as police returned fire. "Treach, I'm losing a lot of blood," cried Teflon as she applied pressure to the right side of her hip in an attempt to minimize the bleeding.

"Just hold on, boo, I got you. You gonna be aight. We gonna make it up outta this shit, and I'ma get you to a hospital. Tef? Tef?"

"Huh?"

"Wake up, baby. Don't fall asleep. Stay awake, you hear me ?" Teflon could feel him rubbing her hair.

"Daddy, I'm weak and it's cold."

"Tef! Man the fuck up, you aight. Shake that shit off. Stop all that mufuckin' whinin' and shit and man the fuck up!"

"Who the fuck you yellin' at, boy?"

"Boo, my bad. Don't talk; save your strength," Treacherous said, moving Teflon's hair from out of her face.

"Don't start bitchin up now, mufucka." Despite her condition, she managed to smile.

"Fuck you." Treacherous smiled back.

"Boo, hold on. We're almost there." Teflon heard Treacherous's words, but could not respond. She was slipping in and out of consciousness.

"Tef," she heard her lover call out again, but still she was unable to respond. Treacherous's voice was muffled and his words because inaudible.

"Teflon!" was the last word she heard before she lost full consciousness.

"Ms. Jackson." Hearing her name snapped Teflon out of her daze. When she looked up, her lawyer was standing outside the holding cell. She raised her sweatshirt and wiped her entire face. Her trip down memory lane made her emotional. She was mad at herself for allowing her attorney to witness her in that state. Out of respect, Mark Stanford pretended not to notice by going through his cellular phone for no particular reason. Teflon made an effort to stand up.

"No, please, don't get up," her attorney advised. "I was just coming to let you know that the jury should be returning in about twenty more minutes. The marshal will get you in about ten. Honestly, I have to say, Ms. Jackson, I have a good feeling about this case. I think the jury may possibly rule in your favor." Attorney Stanford made a failed attempt to counsel his client. His words were more so for himself. This was his fourth trial case and so far he was three-for-three, hoping to add a fourth one to win the case and claiming he felt they would. But in the back of his mind, he was not totally convinced of the final outcome, and his client's uncaring facial expressions did nothing for his confidence level.

"I'll see you back in the courtroom," Teflon's attorney drily remarked, again shaking his head in disbelief about how nonchalantly she was acting.

"Has the jury reached a verdict?"

"Yes we have, Your Honor," the middle-aged white female juror replied.

"Ms. Jackson, please face the jury." Teflon slightly turned her head toward the jury. The judge shot her a look of disgust.

"Ms. Jackson, please turn and face the jury," he repeated. He had just about enough of the pregnant woman's court antics.

"Tsk!" Teflon sucked her teeth and shifted her direction toward the jury.

"Juror number one, please stand and read your verdict." The juror did as she was told and stood and unfolded the white piece of paper she held in hand, faced the judge, then began to read.

"We the jurors, in the case of *the United States of America versus Teflon Jackson*, find that on the charges of conspiracy to commit armed robbery in the first degree on counts one, three, sixteen, we find the defendant"—she paused, turning her attention to Teflon.

"Guilty on all counts."

Teflon's lawyer dropped his head and placed his head in the palm of his hand. Teflon only smirked. She was not at all surprised at the verdict and as far as she was concerned, the juror did not have to finish.

"On the charges of conspiracy to commit murder in the first degree, on counts one, three, thirteen, we find the defendant guilty as charged." Just as the first, the second conviction did not faze Teflon. She had already mentally prepared for the verdicts. After all, she was guilty of the charges she stood trial for. Life as she knew it was over for her the day they had taken Treacherous from her. Besides the life she carried inside her, she had no other reason to live. Mentally and emotionally, she was already dead. There was nothing more they could do to her, she felt. The DA had the look of victory plastered across his face as he stood.

"Bitch-ass nigga," Teflon murmured just loud enough for the DA to hear as the two made eye contact. "Your Honor, the prosecution is moving to impose the maximum penalties under the federal guidelines against Ms. Jackson," the DA burst out, breaking his stare with Teflon.

"I object, Your Honor," Teflon's attorney hopped up and rebutted.

"My client—"

"Your client is an unremorseful menace to society and threat to our community," the DA quickly snapped back, cutting Teflon's attorney short.

"Fuck you, you gay-ass muthafucka!" Teflon lashed out, insulted by the district attorney's statement.

"Order!" the judge demanded, repeatedly banging his gavel. The marshals were now out of their seats, rushing toward the potential altercation, seeing Teflon attempting to raise up out of her chair. "Ms. Jackson, we will not—"

"I don't give a fuck. I don't give a fuck!" Teflon screamed before the judge could complete his sentence. By now the marshals had reached Teflon.

"Calm down, Ms. Jackson," the female marshal advised as she took hold of Teflon's left arm. The other marshal said nothing. He grabbed her by her right one.

"Fuck that—kill me now." The DA put distance between him and Teflon, fearful of what could possibly happen next. The jurors were bewildered at Teflon's sudden outburst and became afraid of the wild woman. They were immediately escorted out of the courtroom.

"I don't give a fuck, kill—ugh!" Teflon belted over and grabbed hold of her stomach. "Ms. Jackson, are you okay?" her attorney was the first to ask.

"Demitri, call an EMT, I think she's going into labor," the female marshal instructed. Teflon continued to scream in agony. Her cries shook the courtroom walls. "Holy cow," Teflon's attorney shouted. Everyone's attention was immediately drawn to her lawyer, wanting to know what had made him suddenly so loud.

"She's bleeding." When courtroom officers looked down, they saw the burgundy stain between her legs.

"Where's that EMT? She's hemorrhaging," the female marshal yelled, seeing her partner reenter the courtroom.

"On their way. Be here in five," he replied.

"Tell 'em to make it two," she retorted. Teflon was muttering something to herself. The female marshal assumed she was trying to say something and moved in closer. "Ms. Jackson, I don't understand you, I need you to speak clearer."

Teflon said her mind. She was somewhere else. The female marshal continued to try to make out her words, to no avail. Just as the EMT burst through the courtroom door, the female marshal was almost certain she had figured out what Teflon had been chanting. To be sure, she moved in closer until Teflon's lips were nearly touching her lobe. "Treacherous I love you," was what she had heard right before Teflon Jackson passed out.

Chapter 2

Teflon awoke with her wrist handcuffed to the hospital gurney. Plastic tubes running from her body to machines, her body was sore. The scenery was like déjà vu to her as she recalled the last time she landed herself in the hospital. Only the how she came about being transported to the facility and why wasn't clear. Teflon remembered going into labor and losing consciousness inside the courtroom. As she reflected back, the thought of her and Treacherous's child came to light in her mind. *Where was her baby?* she wondered.

Then it dawned on her. The last words she had heard before she blacked out were that she was hemorrhaging. Her chest began to tighten and her mouth became dry. There was no doubt in her mind she had lost the one thing that would have kept her and Treacherous connected for life. Teflon could not believe she had a miscarried as she felt her stomach with her free hand. Something didn't feel right to her. She slid the hospital sheet to the side and hiked the hospital dress up over her waist. When she looked down, Teflon saw that her stomach possessed staples. They had cut her open. She instantly became enraged. Not only had she lost her child, but was left with a scar that would remind her for the rest of her life. In the nine months she had the little life growing inside of her, Teflon had grown to love her expected arrival, despite knowing she would have to detach herself from it. Now there was no need to. Teflon became emotionally bothered by the thought. There had only been three living creatures in the world who Teflon had ever loved. One was her mother, Treacherous was the second, and their unborn child was the third. And none of the three existed any longer. With that in mind—just as the last time she ended up in the hospital—Teflon thought to end her own life. The only reason she had lasted this long was for the baby's sake. But now there was no real reason for her to live any longer. Her eyes searched around the room, looking for something within reaching distance to aid her in her departure. For the second time, Teflon began snatching the tubes out of herself with her free hand, only to be interrupted by a loud cry.

"Sssh, don't," the young white nurse said to the little infant wrapped up in the powder-blue blanket. She was so engulfed with trying to quiet the baby that she never noticed that Teflon was awake, let alone her pulling the tubes out. Teflon's heart skipped a beat seeing the nurse holding the screaming baby.

"Ooh," the nurse said, startled. By the time she had looked up, Teflon had ceased her behavior. "Didn't know you were awake," she remarked over the baby's cries, while rocking and patting the infant on the back.

"I've been bringing him in here everyday for the past few days to see you."

Him, Teflon heard the young nurse say. Hearing she had conceived a boy made her smile on the inside. She was hoping to have a son to carry on his father's legacy. "Look, Mommy's awake," she said to Teflon's son.

"He's very handsome," she added, bringing the baby closer to Teflon. One look at her son and Teflon's heart melted like fried ice cream. For that brief moment, her black heart was replaced with a pincushion. She didn't feel like the gang stress she always portrayed. She felt like a woman, a mother.

"You wanna hold him?" the nurse asked, already handing the infant over to Teflon. She cuddled her son with her free hand and looked at him and could see he was the spitting image of Treacherous. "Little Treach," she whispered. Just as she was about to lift her son up and embrace him with a kiss, her room door flew up and two federal agents appeared. "Ma'am. Please take the child from the detained," one of the agents instructed. His words snapped Teflon back to reality. The nurse took hold of Teflon's son.

"Sorry," she whispered with a genuinely sympathetic smile right before she hurried out the room. Teflon knew that would be the last time she would see or hold her son again. On the day she was sentenced to 480 months in a West Virginia federal prison, she also signed her son, who she named Treacherous Antwan Freeman, Jr. over to the State of Virginia.

Chapter 3

Four years later

Teflon had just completed her last set of calisthenics, consisting of twenty sets of ten pull-ups, twenty-five push-ups, and twenty dips. She then made her way over to the royal-blue plastic mat to get in her ten sets of a hundred-count crunches before she made her way to the back for her cardiovascular workout consisting of a two-mile daily ritual that she had been following religiously for the past three and a half years. Since being at West Virginia Federal Institution, Teflon had diligently thrown herself into working out. The end result: She had a built body to die for. Her arms were muscular in a feminine way, and her traps and shoulders were toned. Even through the sports bra and the short T she wore, you could see the separation and perkiness in her breasts despite how muscular she was. Her mid was flat and cut and the perspiration that glistered over her entire body enhanced the definition in her stomach and highlighted the tattoo she now had of the mug shot of Treacherous she had gotten from a newspaper clipping during her trial, along with the words *The Last American Gangsta* replacing the scars she bore from the C-section and gunshot wound. Her waistline was smaller then she could ever recall it being, but her hips and ass had spread like smooth butter in hot toast, compliments of the squats and thrusts she'd incorporated into her workout regime. When she worked out, her ass checks protruded and cuffed underneath with each exercise set. Straight women envied from afar, while gay women lusted from a close distance. They either all wanted to be her, be with her, or be around her, but Teflon didn't allow none of those luxuries. She had made it perfectly clear—or rather showed those who thought it was a game that she was to be reckoned with and was not there to make friends.

During Teflon's first three weeks on the compound, a six-foot, dark-skinned, 200-plus pound manly-looking butch from Philadelphia tried to enter the shower with her. At the time, Teflon was preoccupied with washing her face and the butch slid in undetected. But the foreign touch around her waist and body pressed up against her own wet flesh from behind was enough to trigger her off, instantly causing her to spring into action in record-breaking time. Before the brawny woman could realize she had made a fatal mistake, Teflon had already slipped out her grasp and spin around with rapid speed. In one motion, she head-butted the butch. Because of the height difference, Teflon's blow was delivered to the woman's nose. You could hear the crunching sound on impact as blood sprayed the shower walls. By the time the facility rovers arrived, Teflon was sitting on top of the whale of a woman, strangling the life out of her with her towel. Because of the Philadelphia woman's history of similar incidents, she was transferred to Danbury Federal Correctional Institution in Connecticut and Teflon served six months in lockup, then was returned back to general population.

The fact that "Big Bertha," as she was known, was the most feared and highly respected on the compound, and word had gathered out that Teflon was the one who they had all heard of or read about as being the female who stood trial for the modern-day Bonnie and Clyde case, she had now earned and gained that respect and fear from her peers.

Teflon dressed in her khaki prison-issued uniform after she had groomed up for the day and made her way toward the dayroom. Count for the facility had just cleared moments ago like clockwork and Teflon had hurried to be one of the first who made it in and out of the shower before mail call. For the past three and a half years mail call had actually been the highlight of her days in the women's prison. It had been the letters she had been receiving faithfully over the years that had kept her sanity intact and given her a reason to want to continue to live. Teflon had entered the dayroom just as the officers began pulling the rubber-banded stacks of mail out of the big beige mailbag. Teflon played the background, posted up against the dayroom's wall, while the officer sounded off with her mail call. This was where she had stood day in and out. All the other female inmates became accustomed to Teflon positioning herself to the section by the dayroom door and made it their business not to invade her spot or space.

"Teflon Jackson," the officer called out. "Right here," Teflon answered, making her way to the front of the room. The dayroom parted like the Red Sea as she navigated her way to the officer. Normally in the back, but no one besides the officer ever touched Teflon's mail and that's the way she wanted it. Teflon got her letter and made her way to her room. She sat on her bottom bunk, removed the staple out of the envelope that held it together, and began to read.

I greet you with the highest salutations of peace and wish you many blessings upon receiving this missive. Teflon always smiled at the opening remarks. They had always been the same from day one. No other man had ever made her smile like that other then Treacherous, up until now. She continued to read the letter.

So how is my daughter-in-law? I know it's a question I already know the answer to but it's always a beautiful thing to hear it in your own words. As for this ol' man, I'm as strong as an ox and not just physically, and smart as a fox, sharper then a nail, with patience like a snail. The Creator continues to bless me to live to see and fight another day, just as He is doing for you. By the time you receive this letter, it will officially be my twenty-second year behind these walls, and still my health and sanity are intact. I'm getting closer and closer to seeing daylight at the end of the tunnel. Five and a half more years to go. That's a small thing to a giant like

myself. You know the only reason I speak
about time is not to get you to monitor it,
but to motivate you to beat it. Don't let 'em
win. If I can do it, so can you. We are cut
from the same cloth; same fabric, same
texture. Utilize that time wisely. When
you walk out that door, no matter when it
is, because you will, I'll be standing right
there waiting for you with open arms, and
you can take that to the bank. Smile.

Teflon couldn't help but chuckle to herself. It
never failed. He had always slid a joke or pun in
reference to a bank in all his letters.

Speaking about utilizing your time
wisely, I just finished reading the last four
chapters you sent me of the book. Man,
sister, you sure can write. I know you got
some more for me, so I'm waiting. It's not
only enjoyable, it's also powerful, yet emo-
tional, three things that comprise a good
book and I'm not just saying that because
you're the writer and it's about you and
my son. I know I've said it before and you
tell me to stop saying it, but I appreciate
you sharing your past with me through
these chapters, and for allowing me the

opportunity to know things about my son that I never knew and he would have never offered to share. The two of you have indeed been through hell and back. You two remind me so much of Teresa and me. I know you were thinking about changing the title of the book but I think it's appropriate for it. It doesn't get any better then The Story of Treacherous and Teflon. It wouldn't make sense to name it anything else. I hope you reconsider and keep that. Still no news about the whereabouts of my grandson? The system is crazy. Don't worry, though. As promised, the first foot I step outside these walls I will be on my J-O-B getting some answers. Like I told you before, I gave you my word that I will find little Treach if he's anywhere in the State of Virginia. With that being said, until our pens meet paper again, which in our case will be the following day, stay strong, stay focused, and stay blessed.

*   Always yours truly,*
*   R. Robinson.*

Teflon ended the letter and placed it back in the envelope.

Six days a week for the past three years and some change she had been receiving letters from Treacherous's father. She remembered how skeptical and hesitant she was when another female inmate from out of Virginia Beach had approached her with the letter that was not to her though a letter from the girl's boyfriend who was in Petersburg Federal Prison with Richie Gunz. The first time it was brought to her she refused to accept. Two days later she sought the girl out and found that she'd still possessed the letter. When she read the letters it brought tears to her eyes. It had taken her a week to respond back. When she did, it opened up a line of communication and a bond that Teflon knew would last forever. Sometimes when she read Richie's letters his words reminded her so much of Treacherous. She could see where Treacherous had gotten his strength from and how he naturally commanded respect. She enjoyed hearing from him just as much as she enjoyed writing back. It was him who had suggested she write about her and Treacherous's relationship and how their bond was formed. It seemed like a crazy idea at first, but a year ago, one mysterious night, she dreamed about her and Treacherous's lives from the time they'd first met in the Norfolk Detention Center up until the time of his demise. It was that very same night she had gotten up and her emotions poured out and onto paper. Teflon put the letter in her locker and retrieved her Walkman, along with her notepad and pen.

She had been thinking all day about writing the new chapter she intended to write this evening. Each chapter she had written this far had been emotional for her because they involved Treacherous, but it was the ones like she had to work on tonight that made her miss and long for her other half the most. She opened up her notepad and began to write.

Chapter Fourteen. *For the Love of Riding.*

Bikes all shapes and sizes and colors, from Ducatis, Hayabusas, R1s CBRs, Suzukis to Yamahas flooded the streets of Richard Gold Bowl weekend. Male and female riders displayed bike trucks and stunts, such as indos, burnouts, 360 pop-up wheelies, standing up, and bunny hops with and without backseat passengers. Asses twice the size of mine with mere G-strings and thongs rode on the backs of their boyfriends' and girlfriends' street machines as they raced and performed for onlookers and fellow bikers.

Treacherous and I blended in like chameleons as we rode alongside of one another with our customized bikes with helmets to match. Combined with all we had invested into our babes, they were estimated valued a hundred grand easy, between the chrome pipes, alloy rims, customized seats, and original bodies, our bikes were a sight to see. This was the first time Treacherous and I had brought the particular bikes out. We normally used our R1s or Ducatis when we were putting in work, but because the distance between Richmond and where we lived in Tidewater, Treacherous wanted the most powerful bikes we possessed to pull off the score. Our bikes had parts from the Hayabusas, R1s, and Ducatis. We called them *hards*. We scanned the area for at least three hours before we finally zeroed in on some potential prospects, and potential they had. Next to us, they definitely had the hottest bikes out that night. Not to mention the fact that they had the most jewelry on and most females flocking around them. To us, that meant money. The way these jokers looked there was no doubt they were packing paper, judging by the type of females that lingered in the area. They were posted

up on the side of Virginia Union Stadium,
rotating at least ten blunts in the cipher of
bikers and groupies, while throwing back
cans of Bud Light and white liquor.

It was six of them total. Their bikes had
Texas plates. It was plain to see that the
largest of the six with the opened leather
biker vest, with no shirt on, revealing his
Chia Pet chest and one too many kegs of
beer belly, was the head man of the crew.
Both Treacherous and I gave each other
knowing looks. We had come across hicks
like this countless of times, so how we
handled it would be no different.

"Ready, babe?" Treacherous asked,
already knowing the answer to his own
question. He knew I hated when he asked
me that and did it on purpose to get a spark
out of me. As always, I ignored his question
and shot it right back at him.

"You ready?" He smirked and drew one
of the two silencer weapons he possessed
behind him. I did the same as we rode up
on the small bike party.

Poom poom poom. The first shot Treacherous delivered split the leader's head like
a cornrow part. The second and third ones
tore into his mid in succession like darts

in a bull's-eye. The groupie nearest let out a loud scream only to be silenced by the barrel of my Glock 40. Thanks to the loud music and other partygoers, her cries went unnoticed. Before anyone could make any sudden move, Treacherous and I had already secured the perimeter. Everyone was oblivious as to what was taking place over the blindsided area the Texas bikers were posted up in. "If you don't wanna end up like this fat mu'fucka here you better come up off of every mu'fuckin' thing you got from your neck down. Think it's a game?" Treacherous growled.

"Shut the fuck up," I told the groupie. "You ain't got shit we want."

Out of fear they silenced themselves. Quickly, the other five bikers began un-assing themselves of all of their prize possessions and monies, and started dumping it in the knapsack Treacherous had pulled out. The shook bikers were pulling shit out their ass. When Treacherous told them to put their guns in the bag too, I couldn't believe my ears. "We ain't packin,' he the only one dat was strapped, cuz," one of the bikers volunteered, referring to the one Treacherous had made an example of. Here it was these jokers was out here in VA trying to get their ball on, knowing we played the murder game in Virginia, especially in Richmond when it came to anybody that came from out of state, and only one of them traveled with a burner between the six of them. I had to laugh at that one.

"Y'all some dumb asses," Treacherous spit as he pulled out his Rambo knife. Eyes widened at the sight of it. One by one, he plunged the knife into the front and back tires of each bike. We then back-pedaled to our own bikes. Before we pulled off, Treacherous shot each biker in the kneecap. "Next time bring back up," he clowned the injured bikers and then we were off and in the wind. It always turned me on to see my man in action, just as I know it did the same with him whenever I got gangstress with it. As we darted up Chamberlain Street and then onto I- 95 north, twenty minutes up the interstate Treacherous signaled for me to pull off onto the exit. When we reached the enter section and he lifted his helmet up, I was not surprised by the words that came out his mouth.

"Babe, that shit got my dick hard as hell the way we just took them Bamas."

"I know, my shit was drippin' watchin' you handle them clowns," was my response. I knew it turned him on even more when I talked just as dirty and rough as him. "We gotta do something," he then said. I knew what was coming next. We rode for another fifteen minutes through town before we found an open field. I followed as Treacherous did 120 miles per hour through the open land. Once he had come to a complete stop, he was off his bike, tossing his helmet before I was able to fully park mine. He approached and prevented me from exiting my bike.

"Nah stay right there," he ordered. I took my helmet off and tossed it near his. He leaned in to kiss me. I wrapped my arms around his neck and passionately returned his. He reached down and unfastened my black 7 jeans, then I wrapped my legs around him to make it easier for him. He reached back and snatched off one of my riding boots and slid my left leg out while holding me up in midair, and did the same with the right, Then sat me back on my bike. I hurried, unloosened his belt and pushed both his jeans and boxer briefs down to his thighs. I looked down and saw his rock-hard pulsating. Instantly my inner thighs moistened, enhanced. He hiked me up and slid his hardness inside my wetness. I arched my back and embraced him, all of him. He held me by the waist and bent my back over the seat of my bike. His strength enabled him to sex me in mid-air, having my back barely touching the seat. His thrusts were hard and deep. I know he was totally turned on when he sexed me like this. I couldn't do anything but to enjoy it. With each thrust my inner walls creamed. When his pace increased and his strokes became rabbit-like, I knew my sex muscles had gotten the best of him. He sprayed me inside with his love juices until he had no more left. He was winded and I was pleased. Pleased that I had satisfied my man and he had satisfied me.

"I love the fuck outta you," he said, still trying to gain control of his breathing.

"You better," I replied. Afterwards, we made it back to Norfolk in record-breaking time. When we got home we were both surprised to see that each bankroll the Texas bikers had tossed in the knapsack was full of hundred-dollar bulk no less than ten stacks each. That night we had come off with seventy Gs, not including the jewels.

Teflon closed her notepad and returned it to her locker. Her sex was both throbbing as well as wet. She could feel her inner thighs dampening as she relieved one of her and Treacherous's capers and heated sexcapades. She locked her locker and made her way to the bathroom. There, she pleasured herself to images of Treacherous in her mind. Once she brought herself to an orgasm, she re-showered and responded back to Rich's letter before she took it down for the evening.

Chapter 4

"The library will be closing in ten minutes, please return all typewriters," the law librarian announced. Rich took his ribbon out of the word processor and unplugged it. He then packed up his belongings, turned the typewriter in, and made his way back to his housing unit. During his seven-minute walk from the library to his unit, Rich was greeted with respect by his peers, young and old alike. It was like a gift and a curse, felt Rich, about the amount of respect he had in the facility. He appreciated the love and respect shown throughout his incarceration, but some he could have done without. Everyone that day nearly five years ago, when they televised his son's and his girlfriend's last moments of freedom and announced his own past street activities, every wannabe and upcoming thug or gangsta wanted to befriend him, hoping to find out what he knew. It was the type of attention Rich didn't particularly care for. Even some of the old-school gangstas and bank robbers invited him to join them in their reminiscing sessions of their heydays. Each time he respectfully declined. He knew there wasn't anything he could do about it, that was just how it was. Those from the streets who intended to return back to them respected those who had put work in them and played the game to the fullest, and Rich knew that he was viewed as one of those individuals. But after twenty-two years, Rich had seen the game change ten times over, just from the breed and caliber of inmates that came and left behind the walls that had been his place of residence for over two decades. Through that he became all the more wiser and now he wanted no parts of the new generation that ran the streets now, not unless he wanted an express one-way ticket right back to the penal system once he got out. After all these years, prison hadn't broken him or scared him up. They only made him smarter and more cautious, two things he knew would keep him out in the real world. Rich reached his unit and made his way to the dayroom.

"They already called you, O.G., here you go," Rich's cell mate said, handing him his mail. He was the only one Rich allowed to get his mail for him. Rich went off into one of the unit's quiet rooms to read the letter he had just received from Teflon.

I hope this letter finds you in the best of health and spirits by the time it reaches your presence. As always, it was good hearing from you. You know that without comforting and motivational words in your letters I would not have lasted this long. Glad you're enjoying the chapters I've been sending you. Like before, you're going to have to wait until I write the next couple of chapters because the ones I have now are the intimate parts of the book and like I told you, I don't need you all up in me and your son's personal business (smile!), but I got you, father-in-law. Still no news on little Treach. I count the days down that you're released and hope that you are able to locate him like you said you could. One of us has to find him and guide him before it's too late. Where your time is limited mine has really just begun, so there's nothing that I can do for him from in here, it's up to you to save your grandson. You know it's in his blood so I can only imagine how he will be ten, fifteen, twenty years from now. If he's anything like the three of us, he may not even make it to see that long.

It's because of my mother I survived as a child, it's because of your son I survived as a woman, it is because of my child I chose to live, it is because of you that I continue to fight, and it is because of me that I'm still here. This is all I know and this is all I've ever had. Two are gone and three of us are still here, let's cherish and protect that at all cost. We're in this together now. I look forward to hearing about your reunion with your grandchild and the restoration of your freedom.

Eternal and bulletroof love, Always your daughter-in-law, aka Your Ride Or Die Chick.

Rich folded the letter back up and put it in the envelope. Teflon's letters always touched him in the deepest way. Her words were always so powerful to him. She reminded him so much of Treacherous's mother, Teresa. He could see why his son had loved her so much. From reading the chapters Teflon had been sending him, about her and his son's life as a team, the two reminded him of himself and Teresa. He realized that Treacherous was like him in so many ways than one, especially after reading the last few chapters Teflon had sent him days ago. Prior to reading pages entailing his son's life, Rich had no clue Treacherous had acquired a passion and love for motorcycles just as he had. He also hadn't known that Treacherous had inherited his passion and love for robbing the way he had previously to taking down the same banks. One caper he had read about his son and female partner had pulled off put him in the state of mind of a stickup he had committed while Treacherous's mother was with him. Rich chuckled to himself and strolled down memory lane for a brief moment.

"Rich, where are you going?" Teresa asked, coming out or the bathroom in her sheer black nightgown. Rich had just checked his two revolvers and slipped on his burgundy leather blazer. "Steppin' out for a minute. I'll be back shortly," he replied. Teresa could tell by the way he avoided eye contact with her and kept his back toward her that he was going out to "work," as he referred to it as. She knew that he knew. One look into his eyes and she saw right through his words. "I thought you were going to take off this weekend, baby," she reminded him. Rich contemplated on making up something, but knew it would be pointless. Especially when Teresa already had a suspicion of where he was headed and what he intended to do. "I'm bored,

*just gonna shoot over to the juke joint in New-
port News and see if anything happenin' on that
end of town."* Teresa was full aware of what see
if anything happening *meant. That was Rich's
way of saying he was going to see if someone
was out worth robbing. "I'm going with you,
then,"* Teresa announced, already slipping into
a pair of jeans and throwing on a tube top.

"Mama, I'm taking the bike," Rich shot back.
He knew how much Teresa hated riding on the
back of his Kawasaki.

"So I don't care, I'm still going." Rich knew
it was useless to argue with her when her mind
was made up. He shook his head, snatched up
his helmet, and made his way to the front door.

*"And I'll go in to see if anything is happenin'
tonight. If it is then, I'll bring them out, you stay
outside,"* Teresa told him, snatching up the other
helmet. Again, Rich said nothing, but smiled
to himself. Richie Gunz lurked in the darkness
on his pearl machine, awaiting Teresa's exit
out of the Newport News saloon. He checked
his watch for the fifth time. Teresa had been
in the bar for over an hour now. He was not in
the least bit worried, but anxious. He knew if
she had stayed in the establishment that long
then she had locked in on a potential jook. The
door of the juke joint flew open and Rich saw

Teresa exiting the bar holding up a six feet four, light-skinned brother with good, wavy hair, a butterfly-collar paisley shirt, blue jeans too tight for Richie's taste, and brown cowboy boots, who was slightly staggering. Rich noticed he had stumbled out the door and nearly lost his balance. But what caught his eyes the most was the man's hand constantly sliding down, trying to rest on Teresa's ass. Richie's blood boiled like Iowa about to erupt out of a volcano at the sight. As if Teresa could read Rich's mind, she put her hand up for only him to see and signal for him to remain at bay. Rich laughed because he had already drew his turns and was about to swarm down on the john. Rich watched as Teresa escorted the man to his assumed vehicle. Rich's demeanor changed when he saw where Teresa and the man had stopped. Rich wasted no time making his way over to where they stood now.

"Beautiful, I told you I got it. I'm good," the tall, light-skinned brother slurred. "Let me ride me at my place." He laughed at his own joke, reaching for his Harley-Davidson keys Teresa had taken out of his hands.

"No, big boy, you had one too many, I got this," she said. "I don't wanna die before I get to enjoy you," she added seductively. Teresa could see

the lust tap dancing in the tall, light-skinned brother's eyes as he took in her words.

"That sounds good to me, sweetness, I stay out in Virginia Beach, on the beachfront, can you get me there?"

"No problem honey," Teresa answered, hopping on the Harley. The tall, light-skinned brother admired the way Teresa's ass spread on the seat of his machine. He envisioned his erection pressing up against what he knew to be soft bottom as he attempted to straddle his pride and joy. Just as he raised his left leg, he was knocked off balance by a sudden blow to the side of the head. Instantly, he went tumbling down, crashing onto the pavement. He never knew what hit him. That is until, he looked up and saw Rich towering over him.

"Hey, man what's your problem," the light-skinned brother snapped.

"You, you pretty muthatfucka!" Rich barked, shoving one of his twin revolvers in the victim's face, tucking his other one.

"What I do?" he asked innocently.

"Shut the fuck up," Rich ordered. "Baby, hold this, he move you know what to do." The light-skinned brother saw that Rich was talking to the pretty sister with the big butt he intended to bed down the evening. "Ain't this about a

bitch. You stankin' ass—" He never got to finish his sentence.

"Lights out nigga." Rich brought the butt of his gun crashing down on the light-skinned brother's temple. He relieved him of the four gold chains and medallion from around his neck, his nugget watch, and three link bracelets, along with a wad of cash he later found out to be 3,500 dollars. "Baby, follow me on my bike," Rich instructed Teresa. He handed her his keys and hopped on the Harley. Rich drove until he reached Chesapeake Park. As much as he liked the experience hog, he knew he couldn't keep it. Besides, it wasn't about the motorcycle; Rich wanted to make a statement. He knew how bike owners felt about their machines, He wanted to disrespect something he knew the light-skinned loved just as he disrespected someone Rich loved. Teresa watched as Rich unloaded both of his revolvers into the Harley-Davidson. She knew the reason behind destroying the bike. It was times like this that made her love him the way she did. That night they made love until the exhausted themselves and fell asleep.

Rich snapped out of his trance, hearing the officer's thunderous voice call count. He made his way to his assigned area to prepare for count time, anticipating it to clear so he could write Teflon back.

Chapter 5

Teflon's stopwatch beeped, indicating that she had completed her two-mile jog around the facility's track. She walked an additional two laps to cool her body as she took in the sounds of Akinyele's throwback cut "Gangsta Bitch" on her Walkman. As she walked, she noticed a short, petite, charcoal-complexioned female staring at her the first time she passed by. The girl seemed vaguely familiar to her, but she couldn't put her finger on why. She knew it wasn't from the compound, because she made it her business to lock in any and all faces to be on the safe side, due to all the dirt she and Treacherous had done on the streets. This girl's face was a new one to the women's prison. Teflon had actually remembered when the girl had come in six weeks back. Thinking back, she was almost certain that the little girl had ice-grilled her for a split second, seeing the familiar look on her face now. Rather than speculate or wait, Teflon approached the girl. Teflon's sudden approach caught the girl off guard. Teflon saw that her entire facial expression had gone from hardcore to marshmallow-type. That caused Teflon to downplay the situation.

"Where do I know you from?" Teflon asked, pulling the earbuds out of her lobes.

"Probably from Norfolk, I'm from Tidewater," the dark-skinned girl replied. Hearing where the girl was from put Teflon on point, though the girl didn't seem like too much of a threat, but that's where Treacherous was from and she remembered how he had terrorized his area. Besides, Teflon was not the type to have female friends or any friends, for that matter. In their line of work both she and Treacherous kept their circles very small and even tighter.

"Why would you think I know you from there?" Teflon questioned, watching the girl carefully.

"You're Teflon, right?"

"Yeah. And?"

"Well, I know you ride bikes and I ride too. Remember seeing you out there at the Afram Fest some years back," she confessed in a calm manner, but Teflon saw right through the front. She knew the last time she had visited the historical Afram Festival and why, but still she couldn't figure where the girl fit into the equation and for the life of her couldn't place her anywhere at the scene that night. She was normally good with faces, but this one just wasn't registering. Nonetheless, she grew tired of the back-and-forth with the dark-skinned girl and decided to put an end to it.

"You didn't see me at the fuckin' Afram and you damn sure don't know me, so what the fuck's your problem?"

"You bitch!" the dark-skinned girl roared just as she slipped a jailhouse-made knife down and out from under the sleeve of her sweatshirt and launched an attack against Teflon. Her slowness and inexperience caused her to fail in the attempt and allowed Teflon to capitalize off it. Teflon sidestepped the dark-skinned girl and faded like the Matrix. The girl spun back around as quickly as she could, only to be met with Teflon's razor blade she had now spit out of her mouth. Out of nowhere she slashed the five-foot dark-skinned girl across the forehead with the blade. The girl went down from the blow, clasping her forehead with both hands. Teflon was tempted to continue her attack, but was not in the mood to get sent to solitary confinement. Instead, she inconspicuously trotted off, leaving the girl rolling in her own blood. Teflon had already showered and re-dressed by the time the code on the compound was called. The compound was locked down, everyone was instructed to report to their assigned housing, and a full body search was conducted on all females in the facility, to no avail. Teflon was surprised and respected the fact the dark-skinned girl hadn't snitched. Because she hadn't told on who committed the assault on her, the dark-skinned girl was taken into protective custody. Later, word had gotten out that she was the baby's mother of an ex-baller from New Jersey by the name of Brickz that had been found murdered during Afram weekend after leaving with some biker chick from Club Reign. Teflon remembered the incident all too well and was not mad at all at the dark-skinned girl for trying to ride out for her child's father. There was no doubt in her mind that had it been her in those shoes she would have done the same, only she would have been successful in her revenge, a confident Teflon was sure of. Apparently the girl hadn't done her homework, thought Teflon. It was evident to her that the girl had no clue or way of knowing that she had tried to ride on a chick not to be fucked with. Teflon laughed to herself. She couldn't wait to write Rich back and tell and made a mental note to include the incident in her memoir.

Chapter 6

"You have a prepaid call from a federal correctional facility. To refuse this call please hang up. To accept this call dial five now."

Rich could hear the painful cough coming through the phone before he was able to speak a word. He waited until his only friend was done.

"What the hell took you so long?" O.G. complained as the cough faded. Just as he was to Rich, Rich was also his only friend.

"You know I don't like talking on these people phones," Rich replied. "I'm just checking in, that's all."

"If that's why you called then you could've saved your money, 'cause everything's smooth sailing on this end," O.G. shot back.

Rich smiled. For as long as he could remember O.G. had always been like that, having a never-let-'em-see-you-sweat type of attitude. He and O.G. had known one another for over forty years, long enough to know that O.G. was short

for Orlando Goines and not just Original Gangster like everyone in the streets assumed. Being
twelve years Rich's senior, O.G. was not only his
friend, but also like father figure to him. It was
O.G. who had actually showed him the ropes of
the streets when he had taken them on full time.
It was O.G. who, outside of his mother, knew
what he had done to his father. It was with
O.G. that he had committed his first murder.
It was O.G. who had even schooled him on a lot
when it came to the way he had raised Treacherous in the absence of Teresa, and it was O.G.
who had been doing the time with him since he
had caught the bank robbery charge. The two of
them had an extensive history beyond belief.

"This is me you talking to, Orlando," Rich
addressed O.G.

"Sucka if I could get through this phone I'd
kick yo' ass for callin' me that jive-ass name,"
O.G. spat through coughs.

"You'd probably pass out before you get to me,"
Rich chuckled.

"You probably right." O.G. returned the laugh.

"Seriously, friend, talk to me. What did the doc
say?" Rich's tempo changed.

O.G. let out a deep sigh. "That cracker don't
know what the hell he's talking about."

Whenever he tried to downplay a situation Rich knew it was something serious, but still, he didn't want to push his friend.

"They never do when it comes to us, but what did he say?"

"That's just it. The muthafucka didn't say nuthin'. Not shit I wanted to hear anyway."

Getting something out of O.G. was like pulling teeth, knew Rich. His beating around the bush furthermore let Rich know that it was more serious then he imagined. To him, O.G. was the one person he thought would outlive him, despite their age disparity. To think that would not be the case was unimaginable for Rich, but might very well be the reality. Either way, Rich wanted to know.

"What did the cocksucker say?" Rich tried a different approach on his friend.

"That white-faced nigga gonna tell me there's nuthin' they can do for me. I started to shove my pistol in his goddamn mouth and tell 'em to check that shit again, but I played it cool and told him to kiss my black ass and left out."

Although it was no laughing matter, Rich couldn't help but to let out a slight chuckle, imagining his friend's reaction to the doctor's words. But he sympathized with O.G.

"How the hell is he gonna say that when I know cases of colon cancer where niggas done got treated and still kickin'?"

There was a brief pause. "It ain't just colon cancer no more, Gunz," O.G. stated.

"He said I took too long and the shit spread. I didn't wanna tell you 'cause you didn't need this shit on your mental, but you all I got and you deserve to know. I'm fucked up out here, baby boy. My whole right side locked up on me. I told the doc to give it to me raw with no cut and he said it's just a matter of time before this ragged-ass disease start eatin' at my brain."

"Damn, O.G." was the only thing Rich could muster up. He felt as if someone had just plunged a knife into his heart. The fact that when he walked out of the place that would have been his home for nearly thirty years and not be able to see the one person who rode with him day for day bothered Rich. For the first time in his life Rich felt alone. In just a few more years he would be a free man and the reality had set in that he had no one to go home to. He started going down the list in his head of those who'd he'd lost. Before prison there was his one true love, Teresa; during prison there was his son Treacherous, and now O.G. Rich's mind began to drift into time. His thoughts began to take him back to the last time he had seen Teresa before she had died giving birth to his son. Images of her on the operating table hemorrhaging invaded his mind. His thoughts then flashed to the day he stood in the dayroom of the federal facility and watched on television as his son chose his final fate by holding court on the interstate. Rich revisited the uneventful day he'd been carrying with him since that day.

"We now bring you live footage from Julie Sanchez of the actual chase. Hey Julie, what do you have for us?"

"Hello, Bob. As you can see, police are in a massive pursuit of a brand-new all-black six hundred CLS Mercedes-Benz. Suspects are believed to be armed and dangerous. So far, all we know is that suspects entered onto Highway two-sixty-four westbound, coming off the ramp, headed toward the Virginia Beach area. It has been confirmed, Bob, that there are two occupants inside the vehicle, both African American: one male, the other female. Our sources who have been following the incident since it erupted, tell us that the driver has been identified as thirty-year-old Treacherous Freeman, from the Tidewater Park area in

Norfolk, and thirty-year-old Teflon Jackson, from the Georgetown section of Chesapeake. Sources also say Ms. Jackson may have been injured at the actual scene. Though the actual count has not been confirmed, we are told that Mr. Freeman allegedly shot and possibly killed several officers and pedestrians during the horrendous gun battle, fleeing the scene of the crime while many others were wounded. The emergency medical team is tending to those who were fortunate to have survived this unbelievable tragedy. As far as we know no one was injured inside. Both Mr. Freeman and Ms. Jackson have criminal histories. Police authorities continue to pursue the two suspects, who seem as if they have no intentions on giving up at this time. We'll keep you updated as this tragic story continues to unfold here on Highway two-sixty-four. This is Julie Sanchez, live from WAVY Ten. Back to you, Bob."

"Thanks, Julie. Keep us posted. In other news, two teens were gunned down in the parking lot of a local McDonald's on Princess Ann Boulevard. Hold on—this just came in. Our sources have found out that the black Mercedes-Benz CLS that police had been in pursuit of just hours ago had been reported stolen earlier today. It has now been confirmed that the CLS six hundred Mercedes belonged to a Marcus Bullock of Brooklyn, New York. Mr. Bullock and another teen were gunned down in front of a local McDonald's on Princess Ann Boulevard, after being carjacked by Mr. Freeman and Ms. Jackson. The local authorities have confirmed the connection between the McDonald's murders and the bank robbery. Our sources also tell us that Mr. Freeman's father, a Mr. Richard Freeman, was convicted over seventeen years ago for single-handedly robbing the same bank for over a million dollars. He is currently serving a thirty-year sentence in Petersburg Federal Institution."

Everyone in the dayroom turned and looked at Rich, who continued watching the TV.

"Although this hasn't been confirmed, it is believed to be true that Mr. Freeman and Ms. Jackson took close to two million dollars. Hold on, I've just been told there have been some new developments in our top story. Julie, are you there?"

"Yeah, Bob, as you can see, the pursuit has come to an end. Police have the entire highway shut down. After reaching the Virginia Beach exit, the SUV stopped shortly thereafter on the ramp. Our sources tell us that Mr. Freeman and Ms. Jackson were ordered to throw *out their weapons along with the vehicle keys, and they complied. We've also been told the officer in charge instructed the occupants to exit the vehicle. Apparently, this is what authorities are waiting for to take the suspects into custody. Hold on—the driver door just opened. Oh, my god! As you can see, one of the suspects has opened fire on the authorities. It appears to be Mr. Freeman who is the actual gunman. There has been no sign of Ms. Jackson, but Mr. Freeman continues to attack authorities, as they are under rapid fire. I can't believe this is actually happening. For those of you who have just tuned in, this is live coverage of the shootout between one of the alleged bank robbers of Bank of America and the authorities. Wait! Something seems to be happening. Police are running toward the Mercedes."*

Rich watched as his son was gunned down on live television. He hadn't shed a tear up until now since the last he had seen his son on a visit, but as he continued to listen to the anchorman his face moistened.

"It's been confirmed this disastrous incident has ended in tragedy. Six state police and four federal agents were killed in the line of fire, five others were wounded. Mr. Treacherous Freeman was shot and killed during the horrendous *shooting. Miraculously, Ms. Teflon Jackson was found unconscious with a bullet-inflicted wound inside the vehicle, but our sources say she is not expected to make it. The money was recovered inside of the Mercedes. What drove a young man to such a tragic ending, no one knows but that man himself. This is Julie Sanchez, live from WAVY TV Ten."*

"You have one minute remaining," was what snapped Rich out of his trip down memory lane.

"O.G. It's almost count time. I'ma call you back after it clears."

"Don't bother, Gunz. I sent you some things in the mail. You should get 'em tomorrow or the next day. Call me then and we'll discuss 'em."

"Fair enough," Rich answered, respecting his wishes. The phone cut off before he could get to ask O.G. what he had sent him. He was tempted to call back after the prison head count cleared to find out, but sided against it. Something in the way O.G. had informed him of the mail he intended to receive just didn't sit right with Rich. As he walked to his area, Rich wondered what it could be he was expecting.

Chapter 7

It was two in the morning and Teflon could not sleep. She had been tossing and turning all night. Today was March 3. To many that day was just an ordinary one, but to Teflon it was more then that. Today was the anniversary of Treacherous's birthday and she could not stop thinking about him, which was nothing new, but today was different. It was this date that made it possible for the two of them to ever meet. Images of him and her invaded her sleep. As usual, whenever she thought of Treacherous, Teflon pulled out her pen and pad from underneath her mattress and turned on her night-light. She had intended to start on the chapter she had in mind sometime throughout the course of the day but decided now was as good of a time as any. She opened the spiral notepad up and began to put her thoughts on paper.

"Memorial Weekend," she named the chapter.

The entire week leading up to Memorial Day weekend was an unforgettable one for me and Treacherous. A lot was going on during that time. This was the first time the two of us had actually utilized assistance outside of ourselves. Although everyone within the seven cities knew how we got down, no one ever knew our business, but it was Treacherous's decision and I rode with him on his call. I knew it took a lot for him to ask for help or accept it, so if he agreed to it then he had definitely thought it thoroughly through.

"Treach, did that call come through yet?" I asked.

"Not yet boo, still waitin' on this joker. If he don't reach out to me by tomorrow then I'm gonna hit him 'cause I don't wanna blow this opportunity down Bike Week. I rather have something definite set up versus us freestylin' tryin'a find a lick."

The joker Treacherous was referring to was a guy by the name of Pete, originally from New Jersey, but got into some trouble when he was a juvenile and ended up in the Norfolk Detention Center. He normally despised Northerners but said Pete was an exceptional to the rules because he had strong Southern ties. His family migrated from South Carolina and Virginia to the north, but a great deal of them were still in the south, which kept him coming down. Treacherous said I knew him from when we were in there. Back then, and now there was only one nigga I had eyes for or even paid attention to, anyone else was of no importance to me and he knew it. Treacherous had told me that out of all of the fights throughout the years he had served in the youth facility, Pete was the only one he had given him a run for his money. It was because of that Treacherous said he befriended him when the two had run into each other at Myrtle Beach a couple of years back. Treacherous had told me that Pete had relocated to South Carolina after he left the detention center and started getting money out there, but occasionally dibbed and dabbed in our line of work. No matter what the case was, if Treacherous trusted it, then so did I.

"Whatever you say, I'm with you, babe," I agreed.

"Yeah, that's the best route and just so you know," he added, "we're not gonna ride our bikes down to South Carolina. Just to be on the safe side, rather than ride three to four hours down and risk tippin' somebody off who might be going down from this way, we might as well get a truck, cover 'em up and pull 'em."

"Okay," I stated. "That makes sense. And you don't even have to tell me that the truck we gonna get to pull 'em will leave from VA but won't make it back." I could always finish Treacherous's next thought. We were just that close.

"You know it boo."

As we cruised the local area in Treacherous's Yukon, I noticed a familiar face.

"Babe, look right there," I pointed.

"Where?"

"Right there, ol' boy, the tall, light-skinned one with the blue Yankee fitted on."

"Who the fuck is that?"

"That's the clown-ass nigga I told you that said that slick shit to me when we were down by Military Circle Mall the other day."

Treacherous took a closer look. "Nah you ain't tell me that and that nigga still walkin' around breathin,'" Treacherous spit.

I couldn't help but smile at how overprotective he was when it came to me.

"No babe, it wasn't like that. I already know his life was spared. Remember when I came back and told you some bozo tried to push up on me when I was coming from the bathroom, but we were pressed for time because we were scoping out ol' boy and his man from Bad News?" I refreshed his memory.

"That nigga?" he pointed in disbelief.

"Yup."

"Hold up, as a matter of fact, I think he was up in da club the Alley when we were squattin' on them jokers too or either Blakely's out in Chesapeake. One of 'em," Treacherous thought back.

"Maybe, I don't know, but I knew we'd see him again," I said.

"We about to see him right now," Treacherous barked, attempting to pull over.

"No babe, keep going," I instructed.

"What?"

"Nigga, you heard me, I said keep going."

Just as I would never question him, Treacherous did not question me either. Instead he waited until I provided him with an explanation.

"Guess what that nigga drives, babe?" I asked.

Come on with the guessin' games," he replied, semi-heated that I didn't let him get out and take the light-skinned kid's life.

"Babe, just guess."

"A tricycle."

"No, Steve Harvey. A Harley truck," I boasted. Instantly Treacherous's mean mug was replaced with a smile. He knew I was letting him know this was our means of transportation to South Carolina.

"And that shit is gonna leave VA but it won't be comin' back just like his ass," Treacherous stated.

"I knew you were gonna say that."

"We gotta find out where this nigga lay his head at."

"On it, been on it," I told him.

"What did you find out?"

"The next day I saw him talkin' to Gov when I went to go get us some pizza."

"Who, the Ghetto Governor?" Treacherous used his full street monarch.

"Yeah."

"Okay, what happened?"

"I started to get his punk ass then, but it was too many people out. So I let it ride and that's when I saw him hop in the Harley truck. Gov went up in Domino's and I followed. As soon as he saw me he spoke and asked about you. I told him you were laying low as usual. I think he thought I was tryin'a get 'em by the look on his face when he first saw me. You know Gov get that money too, that legal money. I put him at ease, though, and gave him a hug."

"Yeah, Gov should know he one of the ones we fuck with," Treacherous interjected. "Especially since he's always hookin' us up with the free passes to all the major events in the cities, but then what tho?"

"After we ordered I asked Gov who ol' boy was. At first he acted like he had amnesia until I described the dude. The first thing came out his mouth about ol' boy was, "Don't tell me that nut-ass nigga said something fly out of his face to you? If he did he must didn't know who you was."

I downplayed the situation but Gov knew. He told me he was one of them dope boys from North Carolina and be traveling back and forth between here, Atl and SC moving weight. He said when he's in town he's usually driving the silver Harley-Davidson truck with the twenty-sixes on it and got a spot down in Hampton off the Boulevard. He didn't have an address for me but he said he stays in a white house with a double-door garage and it be helluv bikes in the front yard and a few pit bulls in some kennels on the side of the house. He also told me the kid works alone, doesn't have a crew out here with him. Always brags about how much work he put in and will put in if someone thinks it's sweet. Gov said every time he runs into the nigga he got a different piece of hardware on him. By the time he finished telling me all of that his pizza was ready. I offered to pay him for the love but he refused. He wouldn't even let me treat him to his pizza, so I told him we owed him one and knew how to get at us if he ever had a problem. Before we parted the funny thing was he asked were we goin' to Myrtle for Bike Week. I thought he was gonna say he had a problem down there, but he just wanted to know because he thinks we got the best bikes in the world. He said he was going so I made a mental note of that and didn't give him a definite answer as to whether we were. What I actually told him was we were thinking about shooting down to Miami. It's not that I don't trust him, but the least he knew the better."

"That's what's up, you did right," Treacherous said when I finished. "Yeah, we owe Gov one for that, though."

Once we mapped out how we were going to run down on the North Carolina hustler, Treacherous and I sexed and took it down for the night.

The next morning I woke Treacherous to the smell of turkey sausages, scrambled eggs with cheese, home fries, and buttered and jellied toast with a tall glass of orange juice.

"Babe, get up," I shook him.

He was dead to the world and I knew the reason why.

"Babe, get up," I repeated. "I made us some breakfast."

"What time is it?" he asked in his raspy tone I so loved rolling over. It was in the morning when his voice was most harsh. Something about it just sent chills through my body.

"It's seven-thirty."

"Seven-thirty," he growled. When he opened his eyes he saw me standing there in my lucky powdered-blue Victoria's Secret matching bra and thong set, holding his breakfast in hand.

"Yeah, seven-thirty, nigga, the same time we always get up," I shot back. "I knew I wore that ass out. You couldn't hang with the Teflon Don. I put that hard-core gangster lovin' on that muthfuckin' ass last night. Lil' Kim ain't got shit on me. Who's the baddest bitch?" I teased.

"I'ma let you get that," Treach said with his signature smile. "But because you poppin' shit, after we make this next move I'ma tear that ass up."

"Whatever," was all I said.

"You know how I get after a good hit."

And he was right. Just the thought of us knocking off the light-skinned hustler from NC made my inner thigh moisten. The best sex Treacherous and I ever had was after a robbery we had committed. In fact, all of our best sex encounters were after one of our capers.

"Thanks for breakfast boo, I was starving."

"You're welcome babe, now hurry up and scarf that down. I already showered and I left it running for you."

"Did you get any more soap?" he asked, shoving an entire turkey sausage into his mouth.

"Yes, I got you some more Lever Cool Fresh liquid soap," I answered, knowing that's what he was really asking. That was his favorite and the only kind he'd use since it came out.

"That's why I love you Tef."

"I love you too. Now hurry up. By the time you're done in the shower I should be dressed. I already ironed your black V-neck T, some black jeans, and pulled out your black high-top Pradas."

"Thank you baby." After eating one more spoonful of eggs, Treacherous hopped out of bed and into the shower. I just couldn't resist. I made my way into the bathroom, removed my bra and panties, and put on my shower cap. The glass shower door was so steamed up and the water was running so hard that he never noticed me. He was washing his face when I entered the shower. My hand wrapping around his semierect dick made him aware of my presence.

"I thought you were supposed to be getting dressed." He shook his head.

"I was," I replied just as I slithered my way down between his legs. Without hesitation I took Treacherous into my mouth.

"Boo go ahead, why you starting?" he moaned. I paid him no mind. The water tap-danced on my back as I pushed him to the back of the shower, placed my hands on the side of his hips, and continued tasting my man.

"Shit, boo don't start nothing you know you can't finish." Treacherous pushed me off of him. With his hardness still in my hand I looked up at him.

"I'm serious," he said.

I just smiled and got up. "Punk," I then said before exiting the shower.

"I needed that, that shit felt good," Treacherous said, walking into the room in the nude. The way his abs glistened and indented from under his chest down to his waist always caused my heart to skip a beat.

"That's the only thing that felt good?" I continued to tease.

His silence told me he was done playing and was focusing on our upcoming business we had to handle. I immediately got into work mode.

"We gonna take the bikes today since we haven't rode 'em in a few days, we need to open 'em up and make sure they good for Myrtle anyway," he told me.

"That sounds good. Besides, it's riding weather out. The weatherman said it was going to be in the mid-eighties today."

Once we dressed one after the other Treacherous and I peeled out on our bikes as they roared down the block. We jumped on 264 east headed out to Hampton. We weaved in and out of lanes and dipped in and out of cars, then made them bark all the way to the Hampton exit once we got some open road in front of us. The streets of Hampton were quiet when came through.

Treacherous and I glided through the town like two thieves in the night. Within minutes

we were on the street the Ghetto Governor had
told me the light-skinned kid from NC lived on.
Slowly we cruised down the block in search of
the white house with the dog kennels on the side
and the Harley truck parked out front. Treacherous covered the right side while I covered the
left. After reaching the third intersection to no
avail, Treacherous and I began to think we had
been sent on a wild-goose chase. We didn't want
to believe that Gov had given misinformation,
but that's what it was appearing to look like.
My blood was simmering at the thought. I was
actually looking forward to paying the light-
skinned kid a visit. We were quickly approaching
the end of the street. The closer we got to the
end the more my blood boiled. I waved my hand
to get Treacherous's attention, then gestured
that the info Gov had given was a dead end. He
in return pointed to my side just feet ahead.
When I turned and looked, lo and behold I saw
the kennels full of pit bulls to my right. The
infamous white house we were in search of
was the last house on the block and sat on the
corner. Treacherous and I rode to the end of
the block and made U-turns. The dogs barked
aggressively, rushing to the cages' fence at the
sight and sounds of our bikes. Just as Gov had

said, we saw four bikes ranging from a 750 to a 1100, but the light-skinned kid's Harley truck was nowhere to be found. I was disappointed because I had already envisioned shoving my nine down his throat and making him gag while he begged to have his life spared. We did a quick scan of the premises, then rode off.

Once we were off the light-skinned kid's block Treacherous pulled over alongside of the road and lifted his helmet. "We got some time to kill, whatchu wanna do?" he asked me. He knew I was heated.

"I wanna ride around out here for a minute and see if we see that nigga truck before we go back home," I answered, letting my emotions get the best of me. That was not our style to ride around. We either planned or waited our licks out. My answer only confirmed to Treacherous that this was more than just another hit for me, that it was personal.

"You sure?" he asked again, giving me the opportunity to get it together. That was one of the things I loved about him.

"Nah, let's get the fuck outta here," I replied.

"Don't worry boo, we gonna get 'em, trust me," Treacherous assured me.

"I know, babe."

"Come on, let's go get something to eat."

I nodded in agreement, pulled my helmet down, and followed my man's lead.

Chapter 8

Twenty minutes later we were pulling in front of Treacherous's favorite Waffle House back in Norfolk.

"Ms. Janice, let me get two turkey patty melts and—"

"And make sure they clean the grill," she finished Treacherous's sentence. "Son, why do you always do that to Ms. Janice? Now you know I can never forget that. Hell, you the only person that I know been coming in here for over a year requesting that. Outside the turkey melt, you only eat scrambled eggs and cheese on raisin bread, and turkey BLT's out of here," she ran down.

The two of us laughed to ourselves at Ms. Janice's rundown.

"I apologize," Treacherous offered.

"Um-hm. What about you, sweetheart? What will you be having today?" She turned to me.

"I'll have a turkey BLT, please."

"Something to drink, Pepsi?" she offered, looking at Treacherous to further prove how well she knew his ordering schedule.

We both smiled and nodded.

As we ate and went over our next moves, time escaped us. The morning had turned into the late afternoon by the time Treacherous and I finished eating and talked. Treacherous left Ms. Janice a healthy tip before we made our way out of the restaurant. Just as we were walking out the door the sound of Treacherous's ring tone "Keepin' It Gangsta" by Fabolous wailed off. He looked at the screen and gave me a look, letting me know this was the call we had been waiting on.

"Yo," Treacherous answered, putting the phone on speaker so I could hear. Although I loved to see him take charge in any situation and be so aggressive with everyone, I couldn't stand the way he answered the phone, especially when he answered "Yo," but I knew he wasn't a phone person so he kept his answers short. Besides he knew better then to "Yo" me.

"What's good my dude?" Pete greeted. It was apparent that he didn't take offense or had any problem with being yo'd.

"You tell me," Treacherous replied.

"My bad for the delay, I got a little tied up but everything's still everything on this end, though.

I got shit set up real sweet. I'm just putting the final touches on some things," was Pete's response.

"Dat's what's up, say no more, we'll talk," Treacherous cut him short. Even though he didn't say much, what he had was too much for Treacherous and for me. We never discussed business over the phone, let alone how we were going to conduct it.

"You in NJ or SC?" Treacherous asked, changing the subject.

"I'm back up top," Pete answered, meaning New Jersey. "I'll be back in the dirty by the time the sun go down and comes back up though. I'll hit you when I'm in the area and we can link up so we can chop it up more in depths. You know I can't come to VA, but we can meet in NC or something."

Treacherous had already told me how Pete had gotten on his feet by knocking off some dudes for a lot of product and even more money out in Portsmouth and hadn't been back in Virginia since, except for passing through.

"Where in NC?"

"You know anywhere off of I-ninety-five is good for me," Pete told him.

"Where?" Treacherous repeated.

"How about we hook-up off exit seventy-five at the gas station. It's a club right there my man

Big Tex own. That would be good for me anyway, I got a little honey that stays not too far from there in Dunn, I can stop off right quick and check her."

"I know the area, just hit me," Treacherous agreed.

"Yup."

Treacherous hung up with not so much as a "peace" or "one" to end the call. He was rude like that even when he wasn't trying to be, but no one ever said anything. No one but me. This time I didn't. He knew I wanted to, though, which is why he shot me that oh-so-loving smirk of his.

"Guess your boy is on point," I said instead.

"Seems like it."

"We'll see," I replied.

"Yeah we'll see. But anyway, you remember that town Dunn he's talkin' about?"

I was waiting for him to ask me that. A few years back we had ran through North Carolina on a massive robbing spree from Greensboro to Charlotte on down to Raleigh to Fayetteville. In our travels we had posted up in an area with a bunch of small surrounding towns like Smithfield, Benson, and Dunn in particular. At the time out-of-towners getting money in the south were plentiful and we were coming across some nice licks of hustlers coming from up north down to the dirty. They were easy pickings. A few of them we actually had to leave stinking because they wouldn't lie down without a fight. We had worked that area for about a month until some chicks from NC blew the spot up by fumbling on a caper of a three-man team from New York that Treacherous and I had actually had our eyes on. I'd never forget that particular crew because it was the first time I had never gotten past the name of any man I had ever gone after as a potential victim. I remember me introducing myself to him at Club Kamikaze in Raleigh and him telling me his name was Stacks right before he excused himself and never returned. The most we had found out about him and his two comrades was that one was his brother, the other his right-hand man. I saw him once more at Club Taj Mahal when Biggie Smalls had performed, but he and his crew were occupied by four women the rest of the evening. Later on in the weeks we read in the local newspaper and heard on the news four females robbers and the head dude of the money-getting trio were found dead in a trailer out in the country and assumed the obvious. We immediately headed back to Virginia before any heat that didn't belong to us came our way.

"I remember." I grinned, reminiscing. I knew what was coming next.

"Not everybody is gonna fall head over heels for you at first sight, boo," he teased, remembering how the New York hustler Stacks didn't fall for my charms.

"Fuck you." I gave him the middle finger and hopped on my bike.

"Back at you," he returned the gesture and did the same.

"Where to now?" I asked.

Treacherous glanced at his watch. Nightfall was slowly approaching.

"Let's go check and see if that nigga made it back home."

His words were like music to my ears.

"Right behind you."

Chapter 9

As Treacherous and I cruised down the boulevard for the second time that day the end of
the block was nearing. When we reached the last
corner to cross over, my heart couldn't help but
skip a beat. On the opposite side of the intersection there sat the silver Harley-Davidson truck at
the stop sign, waiting to cross over. Treacherous
and I both spotted the truck at the same time
and busted a right at the corner rather than
continuing straight. Once the truck crossed over
we pulled over.

"Boo, don't worry, we're on his ass. It ends
tonight," Treacherous spoke, turning his bike
around.

I nodded my head and followed. We wasted
no time catching up to the Harley truck, trailing
at a nice distance, careful not to alarm him of our
presence or the fact that he was being tailed. Ten

minutes later we pulled over and watched from afar as he parked in front of a local liquor store. Five minutes later he was back in his truck, busting a U-turn in the middle of the street headed back in the direction of where he lived, hoping that was his final destination. We noticed he was so busy with his stereo system in the truck that he never even looked to his left. Had he done so it may have dawned on him that this was his second time seeing us that evening. Instead we went unnoticed.

Since we knew where he laid his head at we fell back and waited, giving him enough time to get home.

When we reached the top of the light-skinned kid's block we could see the Harley truck parked in the driveway. Treacherous lifted his helmet.

"You got your silencer on you?"

I felt the right arm of my leather where I normally kept my silencers to my 9 mm. "Yeah, both of 'em."

"Let me get one so I can take care of the dogs. I forgot mine at home. You just go around the back and look for a way in."

"Okay, but what about the bikes?"

"We're gonna walk them and park them up in there," he pointed to the left, which was a dead end that faded into the woods. We killed the engines and cautiously walked our bikes into the hiding place Treacherous had chosen for us. With each house we passed we peered into windows from afar, looking to see if a nosy neighbor may have spotted us. Dressed in all black made it difficult for anyone to see us, but still we were alert.

Treacherous and I doubled back and made our way toward the light-skinned kid's house. The closer we got the louder we heard the music blaring from inside his house. Perfect, we both thought as the pit bulls began to launch their barking assault, detecting our presence. All four dogs were silenced immediately with the shots Treacherous planted in their skulls. I heard each one's last cry as I moved panther-like to the back of the house. Instinctively, I checked the door handle of the back door. There were times when it was that easy, but this time it wasn't. As I released the handle I caught a light go on, causing me to fade to the side. Once I was away from the door and out of view I leaned in to see where the light had come from.

I saw a tall, caramel-complexioned female with what appeared to be a long, frizzy blond weave down her back, wearing nothing but a New York Jets jersey standing in the doorway of the refrigerator. She danced to the sound of the music in the doorway while she searched for what she was looking for. Once she retrieved what she was looking for, she spun around and made her way to the cabinet. She was actually a pretty girl, kind of like a younger version of the singer Faith Evans. I could see that she had gotten a ginger ale and a cranberry juice from out of the fridge. She reached on the top shelf of the cabinet, grabbed two glasses, then made her way back to wherever she and the light-skinned kid were apparently chilling at.

"The muthafucka's not alone," I whispered to Treacherous, hearing him walk up.

"Doesn't matter. She's in the wrong place at the wrong time," he shot back.

I already knew what that meant. That being said, I took the butt of my gun and tapped the back door's glass.

This time I led and Treacherous followed. Treacherous knew whenever I took the lead I intended to control the situation and he had no problem with that. There was no doubt in his mind that I was fully capable of executing a plan just as good if not better than he could. In no time I coasted through the kitchen and followed the sounds of the music and the smell of an exotic weed in the air to the living room. When I reached the doorway of the living room the first thing I saw was the light-skinned kid stretched out on the plush couch puffing on a blunt as the Faith Evans knockoff danced provocatively in front of him, with a glass of what I believed to be liquor and ginger ale judging by the clearness of her glass and the bottle of Rémy in the ice bucket. She took a sip of her drink and continued with her dance. With her free hand she began to run her fingers through her blond weave. She then threw the rest her drink back, sat the glass down, and attempted to raise the Jets jersey over her head. That was my cue. Before she was fully unclothed I was already behind the light-skinned kid. He had just taken another pull of what smelled like sour diesel when he felt the cold steel on his bald head.

"What the—"

"Oh my god."

They both yelled in harmony over the music.

I had my nine up against his dome and my .40 cal pointed at Faith Evans.

"Try some funny shit, nigga, and see if I don't open ya fuckin' up like a cantaloupe," I snarled. "Bitch get ova there," I commanded with the wave of my other gun. In record-breaking time she complied.

"Yo, I aint got shit yo," he tried to sound tough.

"Aagh!" I smacked him across the head with the nine.

"A yo-yo is a toy, muthafucka. Now *yo* me again and it'll be your last time yo-ing anybody else, pussy," I spat.

"Aight y—. Okay," he caught himself.

Just then Treacherous appeared. I knew he was in the background watching, enjoying me at work. Treacherous walked in front of the light-skinned kid as Faith Evans sat there in the nude, shaking in fear. Treacherous picked up the jersey and tossed it to her. "Put that on," he calmly instructed, never taking his eyes off the light-skinned kid. The girl acted as if she were in shock so I snapped her out of it.

"Bitch, you heard what he said, put that shit on before I wrap it around your muthafuckin' neck."

That was all the motivation she had needed to slip the jersey over her head.

"Big man, what's this about?" the light-skinned kid asked Treacherous, holding the side of his head.

"Don't ask me nigga, ask her," Treacherous barked.

I could see that he was tempted to turn around but thought better of it.

"Go ahead mu'fucka," Treacherous insisted.

Out of fear of what Treacherous would possibly do to him if he didn't comply, the light-skinned lifted up and turned his head in my direction. I could tell by the way he tilted his head to the side that he was trying to place where he knew me from. Then as if it appeared out of thin air the widening of his eyes told me he had figured it out.

"Yeah bitch." I launched a shot into his shoulder.

He screamed in agony and for a second time Faith Evans sang with him.

"Shut the fuck up," Treacherous ordered the girl, pressing his Glock up against her dome. Her screams instantly turned into silent cries.

"I'm sorry," he moaned, holding his shoulder.

"Sorry for what, nigga?" I wanted to hear him saying it.

"For *everything*," he pleaded.

His arrogance cost him another shot. I dumped around into the right leg.

"What the fuck is everything?" I questioned.

"*Pleeaase!*" he begged.

"I'ma ask you one more time," I warned, lining my nine up with his forehead.

He forgot all about his two wounds and threw his hands up to cover his face.

"For everything," he started. "Tryin'a push up, disrespecting you, even looking at you," he added.

I wanted to laugh at his last statement.

"Where that paper at?" Treacherous demanded, growing tiresome of the whole situation.

A clueless look appeared on the light-skinned kid's face.

"Mu'fucka you deaf?" Treacherous smacked him across the face with his hammer.

The impact of the blow caused some of the blood debris from his mouth to splash the sleeve of my leather.

"It's upstairs in the closet in the shoe boxes," he managed to mumble. His mouth was bloodied and I could see his lips beginning to swell.

"When I come back we out," Treacherous informed me. He didn't have to spell it out for me because I was already on it. As Treacherous went in search of the money I got on my job.

"See what a big mouth gets you."

"I didn't mean—" were his last words before I silenced him with two rounds to his face.

I then walked over to Faith Evans, who was now hysterical. "Please don't kill me, I promise I won't say anything. I don't even know him, I just met him tonight."

"You should watch the company you keep," I told her before I pressed my .40 cal up against her skull and pumped around into it.

"This chump had the mother lode," Treacherous said, returning back to the living room with two separate bags of contents.

He scanned the room and saw that I had taken care of my part. We exited quietly the same way we had entered and made it back to our bikes. Once we were out of the area Treacherous doubled back and got the Harley truck. We loaded both bikes onto the back and drove to

Norfolk safely. As promised, Treacherous sexed me gangster-style until my body couldn't take it anymore. That night I had cum eight times to his none and we had come off with nearly 90,000 in cash, a kilo and a half of coke, four pounds of weed, and six guns.

Chapter 10

The next day Treacherous and I decided to lay low. We hung around the house and watched gangster flicks. As usual we started with an oldie. Treacherous had chosen *Hell Up in Harlem*, *Menace II Society*, *Hoodlum*, and *Heat* last time. It was my choice this time and I chose *Black Caesar*, *Three the Hard Way*, *Set It Off*, and *Durdy Game*. We were three movies in when Treacherous's phone went off. He glanced at the screen.

"Yo P what's the deal?" he answered, placing the call on speaker. I paused the movie.

"Same shit my dude," Pete replied.

"What's your status?" Treacherous wanted to know.

"I'm like a li'l over two hours away from where we gonna meet."

"That's what's up, so me and baby girl gonna jump on the road now and we'll kick it then," Treacherous sat up and told him.

"All right my dude, see you when you touch."

Treacherous knew he didn't have to tell me anything. Although I was enjoying our quality time together I knew it was business time. I rolled out the bed and started getting dressed.

"Babe you getting thicker," Treacherous complimented.

I just grinned and continued getting dressed.

"I'm for real," he put emphasis on his words, coming up behind me. He cuffed my ass cheeks with both hands and kissed me on my right collarbone.

"Didn't you just tell ya boy Pete you and baby girl are about to jump on the road?" I reminded him while fastening my bra from the front.

"He'll be there when we get there," was his response right before he spun me around and persuaded my upper body to bend over the bed with a light push of the hand. I looked back at him and moaned, feeling his thick middle finger rub against my clit.

"Damn you stay wet, babe." His tone grew deep.

"Only for you," I replied, reaching back for his rock-hard pole. I guided him inside of me while he spread my ass cheeks. My muscles tensed as he penetrated my sex.

"Yeah, you got thicker," he moaned, sliding in and out of me.

His rhythm started out slow, but with each thrust it increased.

"Yes, right there," I purred.

"Right there?"

"Yeah."

The head of Treacherous's dick brushed against my spot, causing my body to shudder. My inner muscles contracted around his hardness. He grabbed me by my waist, lifted my body in midair, and began pulling me into him. Whenever he did that I knew it was just a matter of time before he exploded. The heavy pounding caused me to climax for a third time. This time my pussy spasms were too much for him.

"Shit," he cursed right before his legs gave way under him. I could feel his juices showering my insides as he collapsed onto my back. I could feel his body slightly jerk and the head of his dick throbbing inside of me.

"Whose dick is this?" I asked him.

"Yours, boo. Who's pussy is this?" he retorted.

"Yours," I replied seductively.

"It better be," he barked. I didn't even comment.

Knowing we were behind schedule the two of us hopped in and out of the shower and hurried to get dressed. Within minutes we were dressed and out the door.

We had already loaded the bikes onto the Harley truck the previous night and packed our bags with all the necessaries, so we decided to post up on the outskirts near Myrtle Beach once we met up with Pete. We were nearly half an hour away from Dunn, North Carolina before Treacherous decided to pull off the exit.

"We need gas and I'm starving."

"Me too." I rubbed my stomach.

Besides sharing the microwave popcorn during our movie time neither of us had eaten all day.

Treacherous pulled up to the gas pump and we both hopped out.

"Babe, what do you want, Popeyes or Sbarro?"

"Nah, I don't want no pizza. Get me two breast and a wing with mashed potatoes, let me get sixty on pump seven," he said all in one breath.

Within a few minutes I was back to the truck with a three-piece meal for Treacherous and a two-piece meal for me. He was sitting in the truck parked to the side waiting for me.

"Pete called, he's already there," Treacherous announced as I hopped in.

"And?"

"And nothing. I'm just telling you. I told him we'd be there in under a half."

Twenty-five minutes later we were veering off on exit 75.

"There he go over there," Treacherous stated. Pete was leaning up against a gold Ford F-150 sipping on a bottled water. The truck was beautiful and had to have been the latest model.

From where we were, he didn't look familiar to me. Even though Treacherous had said he had strong Southern ties, Pete had *Northerner* written all over him. He sported a fitted cap that came down low enough to conceal his eyes, a short-sleeved gray-and-black designer button-up shirt, which he wore open, revealing a long but semi-thin platinum chain with a medallion

that draped down past his mid. He had on a
pair of charcoal-gray capri cargo pants that
resembled too long to be shorts due to his
height and a pair of three-quarter gray with
black G's Gucci shoes. We pulled alongside
of him. Treacherous parked and got out. I
witnessed the two of them exchange manly
handshakes. At this time Treacherous noticed that I hadn't gotten out of the truck.
He motioned for me with his hand to get
out. Pete took off his fitted and wiped his
forehead of perspiration from the heat with
a hand towel.

"Long time no see, Teflon," he greeted. I
was hoping he didn't address me as "ma,"
"sweetheart," or any other title up-north
cats used.

Not that it mattered, but now that he
had his hat off he vaguely looked as if I had
seen him before. I may have recognized
him more but he bore a full razor-sharp
beard that covered most of his face and was
now built like the fighter Kimbo. His beard
was the type of style Treacherous and I had
seen most men sporting when we went to
Philadelphia one year and offed some young
money-getters we had followed up there.

"Yeah, long time," I replied drily.

"You don't remember me," Pete boldly stated. "How could you when you only had eyes for this brother right here." He smiled, pointing to Treacherous. "That's what's up y'all two still together. I wish I could find something that strong," he said with envy.

Treacherous and I both nodded. I didn't like too many people, especially guys, but I liked Pete's style. He seemed down-to-earth and cool.

"I bet you I can tell you something you might remember," Pete then said.

"What?" Treacherous joined. I smiled on the inside. I knew he wasn't having that.

"Come on my dude, you know I ain't gonna say nothing to get me and you to go another round, even though you owe me a rematch," he joked, referring to their last physical encounter in the youth detention center long ago.

"Any time," Treacherous extended. His words could have been taken jokingly or serious because his facial expression was blank, but his tone was mild.

"I'ma remember that, but nah, though. Teflon, you remember the girl from Diggs

Park that used to bring you notes from Treacherous?"

I thought for a second. "Tammy?" I remembered

"Yeah. Do you remember after Treacherous left and you got off room lock and she showed you someone and told you she think she found her Treacherous?"

I did remember. "Oh shit, that was you," I replied.

"Yup."

"She used to talk my ear off about you. I didn't wanna hear that shit, but that was my only associate and she was loyal to me and Treacherous. Whatever happened to her?" I really wanted to know.

"She wrote me a few times when she got out, but then stopped writing. You know I had juvenile life like big bro here, but at the time I was still fresh on my sentence. I think it was too much for her. One of the girls that was keepin' in touch with her put it out there that she got pushed over some dude she was messin' with from Richmond. I never tried to get the details."

"Um," was all I said, not really caring.

"Yeah, that's what I said," Pete ended.

"What's good with this Myrtle Beach joint?" Treacherous got things back on track.

"Oh, it's a go, my dude."

"So who is these jokers?" Treacherous wanted to know.

"They call themselves Fab-five from T-Ville. That's a little small town called Timmonsville, exit one-fifty-seven off of ninety-five."

"So what's the Bike Week score lookin' like? I mean are they getting' it or what?"

"Put it this way. They're called the Fab-five cause they're the five strongest dudes in the area. Their status down there is more on some rapper celebrity-type shit. These cats own a couple of spots through-out South Carolina. You might've heard of some of them or cased a few of 'em out and just didn't know they were behind 'em. Club Spotlight in south Florence, Ninety-nine Degrees, and Hypnotic both out west in Florence."

"Yeah, I'm familiar with all three."

"Well then you know these spots pullin' in nothin' under twenty to thirty stacks three nights a week each, easy. I partied with these dudes outside of their spots and

I never see 'em with nothing under five stacks in their pockets. I went to Myrtle with them last year and they had nothing under ten apiece on 'em. On the low these jokers usually be coppin' like five to ten birds at a time from me, that's how they really get their paper."

"So what type of dudes are they? They're just some rollover types or we gonna have a problem?" Treacherous asked the question I had been wondering.

"Nah, they're definitely not no push-over dudes. This the deal," he started his rundown. "The one named Corey is the hotheaded one, he'll pop off at the drop of a dime. They call him Suicide 'cause when he's drinkin' he gets crazy. He pushed a nigga at a club over leaning against his Charger. Mark D is his right-hand man. He's the one you gotta watch 'cause he's kind of quiet, makes you think he doesn't want any problems, but then later have the gun up in your mouth. Black is the fighter out the crew. He has no problem with buckin'. A few times he knocked a joker out who had a gun pointed at him. If he gets within reaching distance or feel his life is in jeopardy he won't hesitate to try you. Roton is Corey's cousin. He'll lay a joker out for any of his manz, but he'll lay his life on the line for Corey. Kev is the genius of the crew, college grad, computer wiz, chemist, and mastermind of their entire drug operation and legal businesses. He plays the background, making sure the paper is flowing right, makes sure the product is right, and comes up with the best way to handle beef if it comes their way. In some way or another they all are potential threats," Pete added.

"That means they all gotta get it then."

"I mean it's whatever," said Pete.

I listened as Treacherous and Pete discussed the upcoming caper. Based on what he had told Treacherous I really wasn't moved by the numbers he was talking. Treacherous and I had taken risks for less, but we had never put together a job especially so far away from home for the amount of money Pete was talking about.

"So you mean to tell me we doin' this job for about fifty grand or so? But not really once you get ya cut," I voiced my opinion on the matter. Judging by Treacherous's face I could tell we were on the same page with our thoughts.

"Absolutely not," Pete shot back. "I was saving the best part for last." He then went on to say, "That's what took me so long to put it all together. I wanted to make sure this shit was worth it for all of us. While I was up top they hit me on the hip and placed their new order. Initially they wanted six bricks at first, but I convinced them that they should up the order because my connect told me that it was about to be a drought and prices were about to go at least another four or five grand, so they went up and ordered twelve. And the sweet part about it is they want me to bring it to where they're staying in Myrtle. They told me they're staying at the Anderson Resorts right there on Ocean Boulevard, smell me."

"Yeah, that's sweet right there," Treacherous replied.

"How much you charge them per key?" I wanted to know.

"Twenty-five."

I did a quick calculation in my head. "So that's three hundred grand?"

"Yup."

"Whatchu expectin' outta that?" Treacherous asked.

"Something light," Pete answered. "Just give me a hundred and y'all keep the two."

That wasn't a bad deal at all, I thought and neither did Treacherous.

"That's fair." Treacherous shook Pete's hand to seal the deal.

"I play fair my dude," was Pete's comeback.

"Yo, so what type of heat you think these jokers gonna be packin'?" Treacherous then asked.

"Really not too much. Last year one of their peoples got bagged with the hammer on the way out there and that kinda shook 'em to be travelin' like that with bud and liquor drinkin' and smokin' in the whip. They'll probably risk takin' about one with 'em but nothin' heavy. These dudes really about that paper rather then some gangster shit. I mean, they'll do what they gotta do, but they don't go lookin' for trouble. Plus they trust me and they know I keep the heat at all times and they know my gun go off. They got a lot of love and respect for me and it was vice versa until my shorty down there told me how the dudes Corey and Mark D had been tryin'a get at her whenever I dip back up top and stay for

a while. Dawg, if I fucks with you I fucks
with you, that means any and everything
you claimin' is off limits nah mean. It's not
even about them comin' at shorty, though
it's about how they went about," he clarified.
"You know ain't nothing slow about me but
my walk, my dude, so I didn't just take
shorty word on face value without investi-
gatin' the situation. So I told her to slip both
of them the number like she was interested
and if and when they call record the convo.
I was buggin' off these dudes when I heard
'em tryin'a beat my back in just to try to
smash. They was hittin' her with shit like
they'd take care of her if she stopped fuckin'
with me, how she'd never want for nothin',
and how I'm not really their manz and that
I'm not really from down there, they just
do business with me and some more extra
shit. But check this shit," he added. "I tell
my shorty to dead one of them from callin'
and pay more attention to the other. So, she
deads Mark D and starts hollerin' at Corey
heavy. I shoot down to Atl and NC and
then stay up top so they think I'm doin' my
normal. I tell her to feed the nigga some
bullshit about how she ain't fuckin' with me
no more and how she wish I'd just leave her

alone and she wanted to be with him. This nigga fucks around and opens up to her about Myrtle Beach."

"Whatchu mean?" Treacherous asked, not following, but I had an idea.

"He tells her how they intend to set me up and off me for the birds and then he and her can live happily ever after, smell me."

"That's crazy," Treacherous laughed.

"Exactly, so ain't gonna be no happy endin' on this one, my dude."

"No doubt, but if that's the case then why you think they would only bring one gun if they know you comin' strapped?" Treacherous questioned.

"Because they think they got the drop on me, but you're right, they could have more. No matter how many joints they got we gotta leave 'em stinkin' up in that piece."

"Definitely," Treacherous spit.

"No other way," I joined in.

"There it is then."

Chapter 11

As usual Myrtle Beach was bike infested. Bike clubs, non–bike club riders, and wannabe riders from all over flooded the city's streets. Females of all shapes, sizes, and colors rode shotgun on the back of some of the hottest bikes in the land, while dudes performed tricks and stunts or just cruising. Some of them wore G-strings and thongs on the back of the bikes while others chose miniskirts with nothing underneath as spectators snapped pictures and video-taped them with camcorders and cellular phones. The females who rode joined in the festivities of tricks and stunts as well. Some of them even sported other females on the back of their own bikes dressed similar to the ones who rode on the back of dudes. If you were a true rider and had a love for bikes then this was the place you needed to be during Memorial Day weekend.

Treacherous and I cruised down Ocean Boulevard, checking out the scene. As we approached Nineteenth Street we noticed the sign that read *the Anderson Resort*. We locked the location in and continued to make our way down the strip. In passing we saw a few bikes that we considered jacking and taking back with us. The only reason we sided against it was because we had already gotten rid of the Harley truck we had drove down in. For the most part of the day Treacherous and I just enjoyed being among fellow riders and appreciating the many different bikes we had come across. As night begin to fall he and I shot back to our motel just ten miles away from the beach and waited for Pete's signal.

"Yo dawg, did you see shawdy in the light green with the fatty on the back of dat CBR?" the one Pete described as Mark D asked the kid named Corey, passing him the half gallon of Rémy.

"You talkin about ol' girl with the burgundy hair?" Corey replied.

"Yeah her."

"Yeah dat broad was fat."

"Shit I like the one Black got in da room," joined Roton. "Dat bitch belong in *Black Tail* magazine."

"Wait til you see the thangs I got comin' through for us later," Kev now spoke.

"I hope they don't look like them monkeys you had up in here two hours ago," Corey warned.

"Man whatchu talkin about; them chicks was straight," defended Kev.

"Yeah, straight garbage," Mark D chimed.

Treacherous and I could hear every word as each one of them broke into laughter. Unbeknown to us, Pete had a suite reserved at the Anderson for us to better help execute the plan. He had called Treacherous a couple of hours ago and told us to meet him there. We had arrived just in time to see the female monkeys the crew were all laughing about and their man Black disappearing into the back room. From where we stood we were able to go unnoticed by anyone who might have passed by. We had been waiting for all five men to be visible before we made our move. Treacherous was supposed to text Pete once we had a lock on all five, then he would make his call. Another half an hour went by before the kid named

Black reappeared. Treacherous pulled out his phone and texted Pete.

"Damn nigga, you was back there makin' love or something," Corey was the first to say.

"Never," Black barked with a smile revealing a mouth full of gold teeth.

"You probably was back there doin' a lot of kissin'," Kev joked.

I could tell by the thick chocolate girl's face she was somewhat embarrassed by the conversation the kid Black's friends were having about her right in front of her. She silently made her way to the door.

"I'ma call you shawdy," Black shouted just before she shut the door.

"Yeah, call her a bitch or a ho," Roton quoted from an old Ice Cube song.

"Fuck what you talkin' about Ro, dat was some super-good pussy right there," Black spit.

"I bet you hit it raw too, didn't you?" Mark D said.

"Are you serious? You gots to be shittin' me, cut it out," Black replied back.

"Yeah he did," Corey was convinced.

Everybody looked at Black all at once.

A smile appeared across his face. "What? I couldn't help it. The condom was too small."

Once again, all of them joined one another in laughter.

Their laughter was interrupted by the sounds of Corey's ring tone.

"Yeah we in here. Okay, we'll be ready. Suite twelve-eighteen."

Based on his conversation Treacherous and I knew it had been Pete on the other end of the line, but Corey's words confirmed it.

"Dat was the nigga Pete, he's on his way over, bring the money out."

"If we gonna rob him and kill the nigga anyway why we gotta have our money out?" Roton asked.

"Nobody answer him please," Kev requested.

And no one did.

"Mark D, make sure when you pop dat nigga you hit 'em close so the shit won't splatter all over the place and he out for the count," Kev then said, reiterating the plan he had come up with.

"I got dis."

"Black, you and Corey gonna wrap him up in dat plastic we got and get rid of 'em, Ro, you and me gonna secure the money and the dope."

Kev was just about to say something else when they heard the knock at the door. We heard it too.

"What it is my nigga," Black greeted Pete at the door.

"Black, what's good?" Pete returned.

Everybody said their *what's up* and gave their handshakes once Pete was in the room. He had a knapsack on his back, which everyone assumed were the drugs.

"Damn what y'all was growin' that shit up in here?" Pete complained about the strong odor of marijuana that filled the room. Everybody laughed. They all knew how Pete felt about weed.

"You shot out cuz," Mark D chimed.

"Yo that shit killin' me," Pete said, walking over to the sliding door. He stuck his head out and inhaled a breath of salty air coming from the beach.

"You niggas been partying, huh?" Pete said, observing the half of a half gallon of Rémy, an empty fifth of Grey Goose, countless Coors Lights and Coronas, and an almost full bottle of Patrón.

"This what we do dawg," Mark D bellowed.

"Well, this is what I do," Pete shot back taking, off the knapsack.

He unzipped the bag. "Y'all check this while I check that." He pointed to the bag containing the money. Outside of Pete, little did they know that was me and Treacherous's cue.

Mark D looked over to Corey for some sign of approval. They had all actually liked Pete and had to come to terms with what they set out to do. Corey tilted his head. Mark D knew what that meant. He studied Pete, who was focused on the money as he went for his silencer weapon.

"Yeah, this is what I'm talkin, about," Pete announced, bent over on the coffee table, checking the stacks of money. He never saw Mark D raise his pistol to the back of his head.

Blood sprayed Corey's face from the impact of the shot, but it wasn't whose blood he would have expected. Treacherous slid through the terrace door that Pete had left opened for us first and I followed just in time to catch the kid Mark D draw his gun. Wasting no time, Treacherous released a clean shot to the back of Mark D's head from his silencer-equipped Beretta. Before anyone could react, Pete had already drawn his hammer and shoved it into Corey.

"No happy ending mu'fucka," he spat as he blew a hole in Corey's chest. The two shots I let loose in rapid succession caught Black in the heart and Roton in the neck. Treacherous swung his gun around in their direction and pumped one more apiece into them. Pete walked up on Kev, who was now in shock from the sudden and unexpected bloodshed.

"Is this everything?" Pete asked him.

"Yeah dawg dat's everything we had," he answered.

"Good," Pete said, then used his piece to brighten up the walls with Kev's brain matter.

Treacherous walked over to where each body lay and lodged another shot into them.

"Let's get the hell up outta here," Pete suggested, snatching up the bag with the drugs and money once Treacherous had reached the final body.

"Nah, you stayin,'" Treacherous said to Pete right before he pumped three rounds into his face.

Even I did not expect that, but was not surprised. I knew my man had good reason. Without me having to ask, he said, "I didn't like the way the nigga tried to challenge me in front of you at the rest stop."

I had a feeling that was the case because Pete's words didn't sit right with me either when he told Treacherous he would remember that he gave him an invitation for a rematch.

Like always, Treacherous and I made it out in one piece and back to our bikes. We gathered up our belongings, wiped down the motel room, and cut our Memorial week short.

Chapter 12

Rich stood waiting patiently for his turn to review tomorrow's pass list. It had been four days since the last he and O.G. had spoken and still he had yet to receive the mail O.G. had told him he had sent to him. It had been weighing heavy on his mind since the second day had gone by without him receiving anything other then what Teflon had sent. Unable to sleep that night, the next day after he hadn't gotten O.G.'s mail at mail call, Rich attempted to call and inform him that nothing had arrived. Up until the time the phones had shut off for the evening, Rich made four failed attempts to reach his friend. He would have tried more times then that, but on that particular day the phone lines were extremely hectic due to it being the week of Father's Day. It was not unusual for Rich not to reach O.G. as of the past months. O.G. had told him the medication the doctor had him on caused him to sleep more often then he'd

prefer, having him somewhat comatose, so Rich
credited the not answering of the phone to just
that. As he scanned the pass list for his name,
Rich made a mental note to give O.G. a call
when he got off from work later. After coming
to the fifth page and scrolling down with his
finger, Rich saw that his name was on the list to
see his case manager, Mr. Brown, that morning.
He knew the clock was winding down and his
release date was nearing, so he assumed the
scheduled appointment had something to with
his final evaluation, progress reports, etc. Seeing
his name on the list put a smile on Rich's face. It
had nearly been three decades since he had been
in the real world and now here it was—he had
survived long enough to return back to it. Rich
passed the list to the next inmate and made his
way back to his area to prepare for his meeting
with his case manager.

"Mr. Robinson, you may come in," invited Mr.
Brown. Rich entered the case manager's office.

"Have a seat." Mr. Brown extended his hand
in the direction of the chair, which sat in front
of his desk. Mr. Brown was a tall, bald head by
choice, clean-shaved, slender but built brown-
skinned man. He was ex-military and it showed
in his posture. He had army memorabilia
spread throughout his office from pictures to

plaques. Mr. Brown also had framed awards and degrees he had received throughout the years. The picture of him, his wife, and two children placed on his desk displayed that he was a family man. Out of all of the other case and unit managers in the institution, Mr. Brown was the only one Rich had never heard any other inmates complain or talk about negatively. He had a reputation within the facility of being a fair individual and Rich was pleased to have been assigned to such a person.

"How's everything this morning, Mr. Robinson?"

"No complaints," Rich answered.

Mr. Brown smiled. "Robinson, you know that's been your answer to that question since you've been on my caseload."

"That's how it's been for me since I've been on your caseload," Rich replied.

"I always liked you, Robinson."

"I appreciate that."

"I see your time is soon to be coming to an end," Mr. Brown then stated, reviewing Rich's prison folder. He had already read Rich's entire file this morning, but out of force of habit he always thumbed through inmates' folders when speaking with them.

"Correct."

"It says in a few months you'll be eligible for the six-month drug program so once you complete that you'll be eligible for the one year time off of your sentence and six-month halfway house." Mr. Brown had only confirmed what Rich had already known.

He had long ago calculated the estimated time he would do if he had gotten accepted into the drug program.

"Mr. Robinson, you've been out of society for nearly two and a half decades. That's a long time," Mr. Brown sympathized. "In all the years I've known you I've never asked, but I'm curious to know what your intentions are when you get back out there?"

That was an easy question for him to answer, thought Rich. He only had one intention.

"Just to stay out there and never come back under no circumstances."

"Yeah, I would hope so, but what does that consist of?" Mr. Brown knew by his eyes that Rich meant what he had said, but something in his tone made him want to know more.

He found Rich to be a very interesting man, especially after he'd found out that he was the father of the young man by the name of Treacherous Freeman that he had watched on the news some years back during the standoff with him and the police. It showed in Rich's file that upon being apprehended for the bank robbery he had committed, he was a single parent and he and his son lived together. Mr. Brown remembered one of the inmates telling him about the speech Rich had given in the dayroom the uneventful afternoon they had all gathered in the dayroom and he watched his son attempt to elude the law, then ultimately be gunned down on national television. The speech intrigued Mr. Brown, who came from a household with two loving parents and couldn't imagine being raised any different. He always asked the inmates who were soon to be released what their plans were once they got out, because that was his job, but in this particular case he really wanted to know.

"I just want to live my life," was all Rich had offered.

Mr. Brown was disappointed. He was hoping for more. Knowing the conversation was not the basis of the two of them meeting, Mr. Brown moved on.

"We received a call the other day from a Mr. Muhammad Bashir, Esquire," Mr. Brown informed him.

The name meant nothing to Rich. He had never heard it mentioned before anywhere.

He sat there in silence with a puzzled expression on his face, waiting for Mr. Brown to continue.

"Mr. Bashir was inquiring as to whether you had received any papers from his firm. Important papers that needed to be addressed expeditiously, as he put it."

"Are you sure he has the right man, Mr. Brown?" Rich interjected.

"Yes, he does. We in fact received the papers yesterday. They were sent to you by a Mr. Orlando Goines."

Hearing O.G.'s government name caused Rich to lean forward.

"What papers are you talking about, Mr. Brown?"

"Legal papers."

"If they were legal papers, then why was my mail intercepted?" Rich wanted to know. He was fully aware of the institutional policy about mail being subjected to random review or under investigation for suspicious activities. He also knew that normally that applied to gang members or affiliates or anyone who might be accused of selling contraband in the facility such as drugs. Rich knew he didn't fall into any of those categories.

"The mail was put on hold, Mr. Robinson, because the contents didn't go through the proper legal mail procedures, such as having you sign for it, etc. And due to Mr. Bashir explaining the importance of the content, your package was retrieved by the mail sergeant."

Rich had noticed the manila envelope on the desk when he first walked in, but thought nothing of it. Now that he had been made aware, he could see O.G.'s handwriting on the package. During the time Mr. Brown was updating him as to why his mail sat in front of him, he couldn't help but notice him say, "the importance of the content" twice. His words weren't sitting right with Rich.

"So what did my friend send me that you guys felt I couldn't receive through regular mail?" Rich calmly asked, but on the inside he was becoming irritable.

Mr. Brown smiled and cleared his throat. For a brief moment he let silence fill the air before he spoke. He was trying to find the right words.

"The contents consisted of a copy of a letter for power of attorney and a copy of will."

His words wasted no time to register in Rich's mind.

"When?"

"Four days ago," answered Mr. Brown. He knew what Rich was asking. It was apparent that he hadn't known of his loss.

Mr. Brown could not have known his words had just felt like a sledgehammer smashing Rich's heart. It was just four days ago since the last he had spoken to O.G.

Rich let out a chuckle. "You son of a bitch," he cursed under his breath. There was no doubt in Rich's mind that his friend knew he would be breathing his last breath after their last conversation on the phone. He shook it off. He knew his friend was now in gangster's paradise and had to suffer no more. Rich knew he'd miss his only friend, but told himself he'd see him when he too exchanged life on earth for a better place.

"I need you to open the package up in front of me," Mr. Brown informed Rich, snapping him back to reality, handing him the big envelope.

Rich opened it. Inside were the contents Mr. Brown had stated. He unfolded them and shook them out for Mr. Brown, then handed them to him one at a time as he did so. In addition there was a ten-page letter from O.G. Taking a quick glance at the letter, the first line only confirmed what Rich had believed to be true. *By the time you receive this scribe I will have already pur-chased my ticket to the biggest gangster party in history and entered the building.*

Those words alone put a huge smile on Rich's face. He folded the letter back up.

"I can take this, right?" he asked.

"Of course, this is yours to keep also." Mr. Brown handed the will back to him.

"I just need you to sign these papers so we can have them faxed to Mr. Bashir."

Rich put the will with O'G.'s letter.

"I need something to sign with."

Mr. Brown handed Rich a pen. "Aren't you going to read it first?"

Rich looked at him, then took a quick look at the first page of the paper.

In any event, if something were to happen to me, I leave sole control and power of attorney to my only friend, Mr. Richard Robinson.

"I don't need to read it," Rich told Mr. Brown.

"Okay. Mr. Bashir left me with his fax number, so let me get these over to him and give you these back and then you can be on your way."

"No problem."

"And by the way . . ." Mr. Brown paused. "My condolences," he offered once the fax went through.

Rich nodded. "Have a good one."

Later that night, when the day had wound down for everyone, Rich laid in his bed and slowly read his friend's final words. He found out O.G. had left him his house, 5,000 dollars, and a safety deposit key containing what he felt to be his valuables. After he was finished, Rich pulled out his notepad to write Teflon and tell her that he had just lost his only friend.

Chapter 13

It took everything in her power for Teflon not to shed a tear for Rich after reading his letter, but she felt his pain. Outside of herself, Treacherous and his mother, the only other person he had ever spoken about that he loved and respected was the man he had only referred to in his letters as his friend O.G. Teflon out of all people knew what it was like to lose that one person you loved. She was still dealing with her thoughts and coping with her feelings over the loss of Treacherous after all these years. She knew there was no specific or set amount of time to grieve over a loved one and she was fine with that. Besides, she had no intentions on ever trying to bury how she thought and what she felt. She had told herself when she made a decision to live for awhile longer until the two of them met up again, she would carry a torch for her only true love. Rich's letter sent Teflon's mind back to a place where she hadn't revisited since she was a juvenile, causing her to reminisce on the first time she and Treacherous had met. She went into her locker and retrieved a brand-new notepad, sat on her bed, cracked it open, and began to write.

New Chapter—The First Time, she titled it.

Norfolk Detention Center was jammed with young adolescents and juvenile delinquents. I remember Treacherous telling me how it had taken him no time to find position and gain status up in the juvenile jail for young boys and girls. He had been charged with illegal possession of firearms and receiving stolen property. Like me, the judge had called Treacherous a menace to society and a threat to the community and remanded him in the detention center, only he stipulated Treacherous remain in the youth facility until he reached the age of eighteen. To all the other kids who only had to serve a couple weeks, months, or a year or two, what Treacherous had was a juvenile life sentence, so they all respected him for his time. In addition to that, all the wannabe young hustlers and gangsters had discovered that the man they had read about in the newspapers and some knew of and respected was Treacherous's father, Richie Gunz. But what they thought about Treacherous made him no difference. His only concern was serving the five and a half years in confinement, and how he would pay society back for stripping him of his father as well as his freedom. Some kids learned their lessons and went home better than they came in. Treacherous had never committed a crime in his life prior to the charges he had received, and had felt he was being condemned and punished for who his father was and what his father had done, and he was angry at the judicial system. So instead of learning any lessons and going home and becoming a productive part of society, he made a vow to himself that he would leave up out of there worse than when he entered. By the time he and I had met, four years had gone by and Treacherous grew both physically and mentally. If he wasn't doing push-ups or dips, he was reading a book. He had gotten his GED two years prior and began to teach himself by acquiring more knowledge through the books that were available to him, which were mostly white historical ones. Treacherous wasn't fortunate to have someone on the outside sending him any good books, but there was one kid who had gotten in a bunch of them by some black authors and he offered Treacherous the opportunity to read them.

Treacherous enjoyed reading, especially while he was on room-lockdown from fighting. He had told me that prior to us meeting he had a total of twenty-nine fights in the four-year span he had been in the detention center, and won every last one of them. Whenever Treacherous would get locked down, the kid would slide a book under the door for him. He had read all of the books by Donald Goines and Iceberg Slim over and over until he practically knew them by heart. He had his favorites like the Kenyatta sequels and *Black Girl Lost*, but his all-time favorite was *Black Gangster*, all written by Donald Goines. *Pimp* was his favorite of Iceberg Slim along with *Long White Con*. It was through these books he had become more educated with the many aspects of the game. He realized, through the books he read, whether you were a pimp, player, con, drug dealer, or a gangsta, you were still a hustler and you only had two choices: Either you go out there and go hard by making it, or you go hard by taking it. From that day forward Treacherous knew what he was going to do upon his release. He told himself it was in his blood. Treacherous had grown accustomed to the type of attention he received while at the Norfolk Detention Center. The detention center had been his home for the past few years and he practically ran it. He knew some people spoke out of respect while others out of fear. But either way, I later found out Treacherous gave none of them the time of day, male or female staff or resident, no one but me. He was a loner by nature, and that's the way he liked it.

Treacherous had just gotten off room restrictions after being locked down for twenty-one days when he entered the dayroom. He was eighteen months short of getting his release and decided that he would chill this time since his time was quickly coming to an end. As he got his breakfast and sat down he noticed the young females who had been released from the girls' side to eat. Initially we were both feeling each other, but what started out as a natural chemistry quickly turned into a war zone. Eventually when war turned into

peace he told me over the years girls had
come and gone but none had never really
caught his eye prior to me and I believed
him. He said when he first saw me I stood
out from the rest, that I looked out of place,
and he could see the toughness in my eyes.
Treacherous thought I favored his mother
slightly. I took that as both an honor and
compliment after he had told me the story
of his parents. He said it was the first time
he had ever thought someone was worthy
of even being compared to his mother. I
peeped him staring at me, causing our eyes
to meet for a brief moment. I had only been
in the detention center for ten days, but
throughout that short period of time I had
practically seen all the guys that had been
in there, most of them trying to talk to me,
but I wasn't beat. After the first few days
of being unsuccessful, they began to view
me as stuck-up and conceited, which was
fine with me. I had heard stories about a
kid named Treacherous who had been in
detention for four years and stayed on lock-
down for fighting. I mean, everybody was
practically on his dick. I was told that he
ran the detention center. Now laying eyes
on him had me confident he was the one

who the girls spoke about, even before the other girls who knew of him had confirmed it.

While everyone else sat at the tables grouped up, Treacherous sat alone and had been doing so for years. Apparently, would've made a difference, because I had already made up my mind. I headed toward the table where Treacherous was sitting. I could tell he had seen me heading his way because he stopped eating his cereal in mid-chew. When I reached his table he looked up at me. I remember his eyes looking as if he were too young to possess such a pair. They seemed cold, yet wise.

"Is this seat taken?" I asked with the deepest, but softest voice he had ever heard from a female.

Instead of answering, Treacherous shook his head. I took that as my cue and sat down. I could see everyone in the dayroom looking at me as I sat with Treacherous. All the boys who were in the detention center were jealous while the girls were envious. Even the staff was in disbelief. No one had bothered to inform me that Treacherous liked to eat alone and expected him to blow up on me, but to their surprise he didn't. I began to feel a little nervous, not because of him, but because all eyes were on me—or rather, us—and I hated being in the spotlight.

Treacherous continued eating his cereal as I fumbled trying to open my milk. I hoped that my nervousness in Treacherous's presence didn't show on the outside, because on the inside I was a nervous wreck. I had never met a guy who reeked of strength and commanded respect. I saw how he had the entire facility walking on eggshells. My then ex-boyfriend, who was a bitch-ass nigga and the reason why I was in the detention center in the first place, had been the leader of his block, but he was not respected or feared the way I had felt he should have been. I was only fifteen at the time, but my ex was nineteen. As sharp as I thought I was, I couldn't believe how naive I had been when it came to him, and now I was sitting up in jail for him.

I continued to fight with the milk carton as Treacherous watched me out the corner of his eye as he ate. Later he revealed to me that he was tempted to help me, but he just couldn't bring himself to it. That was not his style. He was a gangsta, and gangstas kept it gangsta at all times. Just then I was able to get my fingernail in the lip, thinking I had the difficult milk carton licked, but as I peeled the flaps open, the dumbest shit happened. The milk slipped out of my hands.

"Oh shit, my bad," I quickly chimed, seeing the milk had spilled over the table toward Treacherous. He jumped up just as the milk began pouring in his lap. Everyone saw the commotion and turned their attention toward me and Treacherous.

"Clumsy-ass chick," Treacherous shouted as he brushed the milk off the front of his jumper.

I was just about to apologize for my mistake until I was interrupted by the words that came out of his mouth.

"What? Fuck you," I retorted. "It was a mistake. Who the fuck you calling clumsy?"

All the other girls and guys were now looking at me as if I had lost my mind. The other kids were sure now Treacherous was going to knock my teeth down my throat for the blatant disrespect. They had never heard anyone take the tone with Treacherous the way I had done.

Treacherous looked at me as if my words lashed at him. Before he could even do or say anything, staff ran and jumped between the two of us.

"Mr. Freeman, please go over there," one of the staff members requested, pleading with him while the other staff tried to escort me out of the dining area.

Treacherous knew why they were handling him in such a manner. On several occasions throughout his stay at the detention center, Treacherous had become untamable whenever altercations arose with him and another resident. The situation with me was actually Treacherous's first time ever getting into a situation with a female. What the staff could not have known was no matter what I had said to him, Treacherous would never put his hands on me. Treacherous did as he was told and backed up as he watched me carry on.

"Get your fucking hands off me, bitch," I screamed as I punched one of the female staffers in the midsection. Another one tried to calm me down, only to be met with my fist to her jaw, putting her to the floor. That's when two male staff grabbed me from behind. Even they had a hard time with me. Later when he came home Treacherous would sometime tease me on how feisty and rowdy of a girl I was when I was younger.

"Why y'all catering to that mu'fucka. I didn't do shit!" I yelled as I kicked and scratched all the way out the dayroom.

Everyone laughed at the performance. Everyone except Treacherous. He had never met a female like me and admired my tenacity. He said he loved the way I fought for what I believed in and was able to say what others wished they could have said to him regardless of any consequences or repercussions. He told me about a quote he had read in a book that had stuck with him: *If you don't stand for something then you'll fall for anything.* He knew I was only standing up for what I believed in. After everything had died down, Treacherous went back to his room where he felt most comfortable, picked up a book, and read it. He said that night he stayed in his room and thought about me. Back then he referred to me as the crazy girl who had resembled his mother who just caused so much trouble. Based on the stories his father had told him about her, he said he could see I also shared his mother's same fire.

While eating lunch, he came across my name from the discussion the other girls were having at the table across from him. Treacherous thought the name Teflon to be peculiar for a girl, he told me, but then again wondered who was he to talk about names? His father had given him the reason behind his name and wondered what had possessed my parents to give me such a name. I laid across the bed with my arms folded, locked inside the little six by nine room and thought about how I had gotten there, but I knew the answer to that: From dealing with a little boy who thought he was the man. That and being in the wrong place at the wrong time. The ending result was me being sentenced to sixteen months in Norfolk Detention House for possession with intent and aggravated assault with a weapon. I didn't mind being charged with the assault because I was guilty of that.

I and my then boyfriend were just coming home after having an enjoyable dinner and evening at a popular restaurant in downtown Norfolk. As I unlocked my home and opened the door, I didn't think anything of the darkness as we entered the two-bedroom condo my boyfriend had purchased for me as a birthday present in my name under the table. As I reached for the light to illuminate my domain, me and my boyfriend were met with badges, guns, and a barrage was yelling. Both me and my boyfriend did as we were told and hit the ground quick and fast. When the officer approached us with the packaged drugs and asked the unforgettable question of whose drugs it was, looking over to my boyfriend, confident he would step up to the plate, something he had always preached, I could not believe her ears. "That shit ain't mine. I don't live here. I'm just visiting my girl." You would have thought he was Denzel Washington the way words came out of my boyfriend's mouth. My now ex-boyfriend would always remember how he had did me dirty every time he looked in the mirror and saw the scar on his face that ran from the side of his eye down to the corner of his mouth, compliments of my blade, which I used to keep in my mouth at all times, the way I used to see my mother do before they parted. Far from being a dummy, seeing that the fix was in,

I spit the razor into my hand just as quick as any veteran on Rikers Island and caught my ex across the face, good enough to send him to the hospital for 150 stitches known as a buck-fifty. The police maced me with pepper spray to subdue me and carried me off to detention, while they took my ex to the hospital.

He was charged with the drugs in the house as well, but posted bail and because I refused to tell who the drugs really belonged to and my ex had already given his statement, he beat his case and I wore the weight. I couldn't bring myself to snitch on somebody. It just wasn't in my blood. I was and still what you'd call a ride or die bitch so I took the sixteen months they gave me and maintained my integrity and self-respect, compromising neither of the two. Neither of my parents were ever really there for me or told me anything to prepare me for the life that lay ahead of me, but what I knew about them both, I assumed they played the game fair, each playing their role and position.

As I laid in the bed that night I couldn't help but think about Treacherous. It wasn't my intention to beef with him the way I had, but he had caught my vein. I had an issue with the way people talked to me, males in particular and still do. My mother had instilled that inside of me and there was no exception to the rule. Besides, all that was built up inside of me from my ex was released and directed toward him. It took me a day take it down and cool off to realize I wasn't even mad at him. I had no right to be because I barely knew him other then what I had heard about him. *He must think I'm crazy,* I thought as I dwelled on the situation. I couldn't figure back then why was I so concerned about what he thought about me. I had no clue, but I had promised myself when my forty-five-day room restriction was up I would step to him again, only with a different approach. I laid back in the six by nine room's bed and closed my eyes that night. Images of my childhood haunted me, invading my mind as I slipped into a trance and began to relive my past. After my forty-five days of room restriction had ended I was all too ready to see Treacherous again and start all over. Being in the room for so long and just eating and resting, had put on a few pounds on me, filling out my 112-pound frame into an even 120 pounds, all eight pounds going into the right places. My hair had also grown at least two-and-a-half inches from keeping it in two, but that day I wore it all pulled back in one big ponytail, which showed off my cornrows of good hair. I had actually enjoyed my little room vacation. It gave me time to gather my thoughts, and now that I had gotten them together I wanted to be allowed to interact with the others, one person in particular.

Treacherous later admitted he had scratched my last day of room lock date off his calendar as soon as he woke. He had been counting down the forty-five days they had given me. Throughout that time he had done less reading and more working out, trying to get better toned. He had always had a nice, chiseled physique, but he told me I became his motivation. There was something about me that caused him to want to work out harder. He went from doing a thousand push-ups a day to doing fifteen hundred, along with increasing his crunches from 750 a day to a thousand, adding to his washboard stomach. When he had weighed himself two days before, he had gone up from 170 pounds to 182 pounds solid, with only 10 percent body fat. During my room lock he had packed on twelve pounds of bulk.

The staff was a little leery about allowing me to return to general population, especially not knowing how Treacherous would react to seeing me again, so they decided to monitor both of our behavior, prepared for anything. The last thing they wanted to see was Treacherous half killing me, but I wasn't worried about anything like that. My only concern was that he wouldn't want to hear me out.

All the other inmates had been doing their own counting down of my release, placing bets on how long it would take for me to go back into lockup or get strangled by Treacherous, betting their breakfast, lunch, and dinner trays. The detention center had gotten live in the past month and a half. Some kids from Norfolk had gotten arrested in a drug raid and smuggled some weed inside, and six new girls, three who were young prostitutes, had came up in there, so everybody was trying to get in on the action. Treacherous had later hipped me to the fact that the kids who had possession of the weed had both heard about and respected him, so they offered him a nice chunk, figuring he either smoked or wanted to trick with the young prostitutes, who were giving other inmates hand jobs and blow jobs for food and weed. Some were even taking chances sliding up in the bathroom or one of the classrooms with them unnoticed, sexing the young prostitutes. But Treacherous wasn't concerned with any of that. He didn't get high nor did he trick. He did take the weed, though, and stashed it in a book he knew nobody would touch because none of the kids up in there really read books.

All the girls were attracted to Treacherous and tried to entice him in hopes of becoming his jailhouse girlfriend, by flashing their breasts at him and propositioning him, but he was only interested in one girl. Treacherous sat at his regular table by himself as he saw the young girls lined up coming from off the female side. In total, including me, there were now eleven girls, which was the most Treacherous had ever seen in the juvenile facility at one time the whole four years and some change he had been there.

For a minute Treacherous thought I had not been a part of the female lineup, and wondered where I was, but right before the door had fully closed, he saw me.

I came through the door with that same style and grace I thought sparked the look Treacherous had on his face when he first laid eyes on me, still looking as if I didn't belong in such a place. As I entered the dining area, our eyes met just like before. Treacherous tried to play it off and act as if it were just coincidence that he happened to look in my direction, but I knew better. He couldn't help but to notice how good those forty-five days were to me. Having two good seeing eyes, he couldn't help but notice how I had blossomed into something even more beautiful while in isolation, seeing that I had put on a few pounds in all the right places and how my hair had even grown. One of the girls had noticed the inconspicuous way Treacherous was looking at me. "Girl, that nigga checkin' you out," the girl volunteered.

"Mind your fucking business," I swung around and snapped, irritated by the girl's nosiness. The girl started to snap back with a sly remark, but thought better of it. I con-

tinued to watch Treacherous as he glided
to his usual spot. My heart skipped a beat.
Treacherous sat there at the very same table
he had been sitting at the first time I had
ever seen him, only this time he was much
bigger. He could have easily passed for a
Greek god or a poster child for a muscle
magazine, I thought, seeing the indentions
of his physique through his shirt as his trap
muscles sat up just below his ears.

Although we didn't realize it at that
time—or rather, we didn't give a fuck—all
eyes were on us. Everyone wanted to see
the outcome of Treacherous and Teflon's
reunion. Some kids snickered under their
breaths, anticipating the worse, while
others who bet in favor of Treacherous
humbling himself thought the opposite.
Staff was just ready for whatever way it
went. It was their job to secure the safety
of the institution and that was their only
concern.

I got my breakfast and began looking
around as if I was in search of a seat, but
it was only to buy me some time to get my
thoughts together and decide whether I
really wanted to go through with my intentions, because I already knew where

I intended to eat. One of the guys who tried to push up on me when I first arrived motioned for me to sit with him and his clown-ass friends, but I acted as if I hadn't seen him. I made up my mind and walked toward my intended destination.

Treacherous observed me looking around for what he assumed to be a place to sit. He started to motion for me to come and chill with him, but thought better of it, because he knew that wasn't gangsta, but I could see in his facial expression that he wasn't feelin' when he saw the punk kid to his right try to get me to come chill with him and his punk-ass boys. He told me his blood began to boil. He told me he wanted to take his food tray and bash the kid in the face. Honestly, I would've loved to see him do it. It would've turned me on and just made me want him more. At the sight of me ignoring them and heading toward him, he began to calm down, but had I accepted the punk kid's invitation, he knew he would've gotten up, went over there, and followed through with his first thought just on general principle. As childish as it may have seemed, that's just how Treacherous got down.

Fats was positive I had seen him trying to get my attention and deliberately ignored him. Had he not seen me walking toward Treacherous I think he would have tried to scream on me and try to embarrass me in front of everybody, but unbeknown to him, not going with his first instinct saved him from a crucial beat-down, because he was not aware of what was taking place between Treacherous and me, and could not have known that had he disrespected me like the way he initially started to, I would've grabbed a tray and smashed his fucking face in myself.

Everybody watched as I stopped in front of Treacherous's table.

"Can I sit here?" I asked with confidence.

"Go ahead, it ain't mine," replied Treacherous nonchalantly.

Hearing Treacherous's voice did something to me. The baritone sound made me want to surrender to him in every way possible, but I maintained my composure as I sat down. Treacherous had waited forty-five days for this day and now that it had arrived he wasn't too sure how he wanted to handle it. He was not used to talking to females, so he didn't really know what to say to me, he later confessed. The only thing he could strike up a conversation about were jail things, but he didn't want to discuss that because he was living it, so why talk about it. He wondered if he should start with an apology, but quickly erased the thought because he didn't owe me one when he didn't do anything to me. The thought of everyone staring at him caused him to clinch his teeth. He didn't have to look around to know that they were. He could feel their eyes all on the side of his face. He continued to eat his breakfast, thinking of where to begin.

I thought about what I would say to Treacherous the whole forty-five days I was on room restriction. I had rehearsed my opening over and over until it sounded right to me, but as I sat before him, all I had rehearsed faded out of my mind, and my thoughts became a blur. I noticed all the other girls were staring at me like I was crazy. Rather then black out on them and risk going back to lockup before I accomplished what I set out to do, I gave them a pass and rolled my eyes at them. You would've thought me and Treacherous were playing the leading role in a drama movie the way everyone was focused on us. I knew even if Treacherous wanted to say something to me first, he wouldn't, because his reputation was on the line, so I knew I would have to be the one to initiate it. I took a deep breath and then exhaled.

"Um, Treach."

Hearing my soft-toned voice speak his name caused Treacherous to stop eating and look up. He had no idea I had possessed such a beautiful and smooth voice. On the last encounter I had sounded just as rough, if not rougher, than the average dude in there when I stood up to him, he thought.

I knew I now had his attention hearing me say his name, so I continued.

"I want to apologize for what I'm—"

"You don't owe me any apology," Treacherous interrupted me.

"That shit wasn't about—"

I cut him back off. "Yes, it was about something. I had no right flippin' out on you like that that day. I ain't even—"

"Hold on, shorty," Treacherous interrupted again.

"Yo, mind your muthafuckin' business," barked Treacherous to all who had been paying close attention to me and him, some even leaning out of their seats. Everyone began to act as if they were involved in something other than our conversation.

I smiled on the inside at how Treacherous had checked the whole dayroom. Even the staff began to mind their business after hearing the power and strength behind Treacherous's words. It was apparent that rather than a problem, there was a connection between the two of us.

"My bad, pardon me. What were you sayin'?"

I continued. "I was just sayin' I ain't even know you like that to be screamin' on you the way I did, and it was my bad. I know you got a lot of time up in here and a lot of respect, more than I ever seen one man have, and I wanted you to know I didn't mean to disrespect you because like everybody else, I respect you too."

Treacherous looked me in my eyes as I spoke, and I never broke his stare. Even most of the dudes he had come across who professed to be thorough could not hold a stare as long as I had when I spoke. Treacherous knew I was not like any other female he had ever known. Most girls always showed a sign of weakness or vulnerability, but even in my apology Treacherous detected nothing but strength and security. He was intrigued to know more about me.

"Yo, I respect you for respecting me enough to get at me like this, but that shit we went through is over, just like the forty-five days you just did. I could've handled the situation differently too, but it is what it is, you know what I'm sayin'? We cool, ain't no beef, and if you have any problems while you up in here let me know, I don't care if it's inmates or staff, I got your back," Treacherous stated firmly.

"And I got your back too," I replied.

Treacherous looked at me awkwardly, then shot me a half smile that only I caught.

"A'ight, I respect that."

I shot him the same half grin.

"A'ight, shorty, I'll catch you later. You cuttin' into my reading time," said Treacherous, getting up from the table.

I did not want him to leave, but I understood he had a set schedule. Before I left up out of there I intended to become a part of his daily schedule as well. It had dawned on me that we hadn't been properly introduced.

"Wait," I called out as Treacherous began walking away.

"What up?"

"You don't even know my name."

"Yes I do, Miss Teflon Jackson," Treacherous replied before walking away, but that was the last time he would ever walk away from me again, because from that day forward Treacherous and I were inseparable.

Six months later things between Treacherous and me had strengthened beyond anyone's imagination, and no one but us liked it. Other male inmates hated and despised Treacherous from afar because they wanted to be him while they lusted over me. The female inmates who once thought they had a chance with Treacherous felt the same way, but they knew better. It was no secret that I would hurt something over him. Every so often, a new girl was gassed up or one of the regulars built up enough heart and nerve to step to Treacherous, only to feel the wrath of me, who didn't play when it came to Treacherous. Before my sentence at the detention center was complete, I had received room restriction three separate occasions, badly injuring three girls who tried to move in on my man.

Staff thought me to be a bad influence on Treacherous. Often they tried to separate the two of us to no avail. They even went as far as trying to get Treacherous transferred to the county jail, but never had good reason to because he never gave them one. Ever since I had came into the picture Treacherous had been reserved and humble. He tried to keep me at bay, but couldn't control my temper when it came to my jealousy. Treacherous assured me that he only had eyes for me. To prove it, he carved a set of eyes in his arm with my name over top with the metal part of a number two pencil.

Although I believed Treacherous's every word, I didn't trust other women. My motto was what was mine was mine and Treacherous belonged to me. Treacherous went through hell every time I was locked down. He enjoyed my company and conversation and missed it whenever I got into trouble. We would talk about what we were going to do together when we were both released. The days couldn't go by quicker enough for Treacherous, but they were steadily approaching, he knew. I would be released first, but Treacherous knew he wouldn't be too far behind.

I was on room lock once again and though he missed me, Treacherous was heated with me. He tried to defuse the situation that caused me to be confined to my room, but *I* wouldn't listen, and now after my room lock was over, in sixty days I would be going home and Treacherous knew he wouldn't see me again until his release. Treacherous later told me how disappointed he was at me and had played the tape back that lead to my predicament. I remembered it as if it were yesterday. This incident was inevitable because some bitches are just hardheaded and are going to try you anyway until you show and prove to them. Her name was Carmen and she was from Richmond.

"Hey, Treach," she chimed, approaching the table where Treacherous played solitaire. Carmen was the newest female in the detention center. She was an attractive Hispanic sixteen-year-old who was caught shoplifting in Military Circle Mall.

"What do you want, Carmen?" Treacherous asked, not bothering to look up. He knew Carmen liked him, but he paid her no mind. She stood five feet nine inches tall with still room to grow. Her hair was black with blond highlights, which matched her smooth skin tone. Both her body and facial features favored the Latina singer Shakira. Treacherous later confessed after I whipped her ass that he would have to turn away from her because she would flash one of her 34Cs at him whenever I wasn't around. Once, Treacherous noticed Carmen fondling herself, while licking her lips, which always seemed as if they were laced with M·A·C lip gloss. Even if he weren't with me, Treacherous had told me he was not attracted to Carmen's demeanor.

"You," she boldly answered.

"Get out of here, Carmen, 'fore you get yourself in something you can't get out of," Treacherous warned her. This bitch wouldn't take a hint, though.

Carmen knew exactly what Treacherous was insinuating. She figured if she could be viewed as being just as hard as me, then maybe Treacherous would choose her over my ass. Little did she know she was wrong.

"I know you don't think somebody scared of that chick. Maybe these other *puntas* is but not me, sweetheart, I'm Boriqua, I ain't from around here. I'm from Richmond, the projects, baby!" Carmen announced.

Right at that moment, I was returning from the restroom. Instantly I zeroed in on Carmen hovering over Treacherous. My blood began to boil. I remembered what Treacherous had said about my temper and tried to calm myself. I wanted to spend my remaining two months left with him before I was released. I could see everyone watching as I made my way over to Carmen and Treacherous.

"Yeah *papi,* I bet you never had your dick sucked the way I could suck."

That was all I had to hear to make me spring into action.

Being Hispanic made it convenient for me to grab a fistful of Carmen's long, silky hair. Carmen never saw it coming. I flung Carmen around so rapid and forcefully that she got whiplash. "Ugh," she said as she hit the floor. I immediately pounced on top of Carmen. I intended to make an example out of her as I commenced to pounding on Carmen's beautiful pecan face. I wanted all the other females in the detention center to see what they'd be facing when they got released if I heard they tried to move in on

Treacherous while I was gone. By the time
the slaughter was over, both of my hands
were swollen from the beating I had put
on Carmen, while both of Carmen's eyes
were purple, she had swallowed two teeth,
and was treated for a fractured collarbone
from the fall. The day I was released one of
the girls I knew was trustworthy delivered
a letter from me to Treacherous. It would
be the last letter he would receive from me
before I was released. Treacherous went to
his room and locked himself in. The letter
was folded as small as it could be, taped
on all four corners. Treacherous smiled
as he fought to unwrap the missive I had
tried my best to secure. Whenever I would
receive room lock, me and Treacherous
would write each other and send our letters
to one another through the same girl. Each
time he opened one of my notes it always
started out the same: *For your eyes only.*
That was one of the things he admired and
had grown to love about me. Treacherous
finally opened up what would be his last
letter from me. He had told me specifically
not to write when I got out. I was disappointed at first until he explained how once
we were released there was no looking
back. Confinement would be a thing of the

past. The next time we would see or hear from each other we would both be free of bondage. That night Treacherous told me he laid back on his bunk and opened the yellow lined paper and read my letter.

Hey baby,

I know you're probably still mad at me, but don't be. You know how I am when it comes to you. I told you before, I tried to keep my cool like you always tell me to, but I couldn't let that one slide. That was just total disrespect. That chick had it coming to her anyway. I think I did good, 'cause I never said anything but I knew she used to be flashing you and playing with herself when I wasn't around. Yeah, you didn't think I knew that. Our mail carrier used to tell me. I had her watching you. She told me you used to be turning your head, lucky for you (smile). But when I heard her talking about putting you in her mouth and all of that, that was it, she had to get it. Besides, I'm the only one who's going to be doing that. Yeah, I said it. I can't wait until you come up out of that hellhole. I remember everything we talked about, but by the time you get here I will have already gotten a few things established for us. I know

*you told me don't worry about that other
thing, but baby, trust me, I got it. That
muthafucka owe and he gonna pay, one
way or another. I don't have to tell you to
hold your head in there because you were
doing that before we met, I think that's
what attracted me to you; in fact, I know.
Those eighteen months being in there with
you were the best months of my life, and I
wouldn't change them for nothing. I hope
you feel the same. You better, nigga (smile).
So, this is it, our last letter. Baby it's been
real, and it's gonna get even realer when
you hit the bricks. Until then . . . Love you!*

   Til Death Do Us Part,
   Your Ride Or Die Chick.

Treacherous never responded back to the
letter, but when I met him outside when
he was released that letter was one of the
only things he'd left the detention center
with. From that day forward the reign of
Treacherous and Teflon began.

Teflon closed the fresh notepad after ending
the latest excerpt, pulled out the one she used to
write letters, and began responding back to Rich.

Chapter 14

Six years later

"You have a prepaid call from Teflon Jackson, from a federal correctional facility, your call may be recorded or monitored, to accept this call press five, to refuse this call hang up, to block this caller from future calls press pound-pound."

"Hey baby girl." Rich greeted, accepting Teflon's call.

"Hey," she replied

As always, Rich could hear the frustration in her tone. It was the same frustration he had detected and had been hearing for nearly six months, since he had been released from prison and had the phone turned on so he and Teflon could communicate. It tore Rich up inside the first time he'd spoken to her over the phone.

In her letters throughout the years of their corresponding, she'd always sound so strong to Rich, but despite her trying to maintain that same sense of strength over the phone, her voice came across as that of a woman whose spirits were breaking by the day and patience was wearing thin. It bothered him, knowing that there wasn't anything he could really do to change her current situation, as fast as he would have liked to. Since he had been released, the moment his feet touched the pavement of Virginia's streets, Rich had dedicated his time to the two promises he had made Teflon. The last letter before he got out and the first time he had written to her as a free man, both maintained his promises. One, to locate the whereabouts of his grandson, and two, find representation to handle Teflon's appeal for her case. He had made progress on them both, but not enough to satisfy him or make him want to share with Teflon. Luckily for him, before he had passed away, O.G. had left him enough money to tie him over as well as a place to lay his head until he got on his feet, or else it would have been that much more difficult to do anything for Teflon or himself, for that matter. Rich often wondered what it would have been like for him, at his age, coming home to nothing. As the thought crossed his mind, Rich shook it off and refocused on his phone call

"I see you got the money I sent to put on the phone."

"Yeah, thanks, but the rest I could've did without," Teflon retorted, referring to the additional 200 dollars Rich had sent her for herself on top of the 200 he sent for the phone.

"What I tell you about talkin' crazy," he shot back. He knew she was going to say something about the extra money. Since he'd been home, he had sent her money for the phone and prison necessities.

"And don't try to send it back either, like you did before, 'cause I'ma send it right back."

That got a slight chuckle out of Teflon.

"You think you know me, ol' man?"

Rich always smiled at the title he had grown accustomed to.

"I think I've known you long enough to say I do, wouldn't you say?"

"You already know the answer to that," Teflon replied.

Rich expected as much. He was used to not getting straight answers from Teflon when it came to questions about how close they'd become throughout the nine and a half years they'd bonded.

"I love you too, daughter-in-law," he offered.

It was Teflon's turn to smile.

Hearing those words coming from Rich were always comforting to her. Whenever he addressed her as daughter-in-law, it always caused her to think about Treacherous and how legally she would have been Rich's daughter-in-law had his son still been alive. She reflected back on the first time she and Rich had spoken on the phone. She couldn't believe her ears. Had she not known better she would have sworn that it was Treacherous she was actually speaking with. Their voices were almost identical, sharing the same baritone but raspy voice. It took some getting used to for her in the beginning. Talking to Rich was very emotional for Teflon at first. It was if Treacherous had been reincarnated, but after awhile she began to notice the difference. Where Rich's voice became subtle, at times Treacherous had always remained hard even in the midst of expressing himself. Both men spoke with conviction and passion, but Rich's words were those of a much wiser man with an older soul. His experience in life revealed itself in their conversations. Every so often, Rich would say something that sounded as if he were quoting Treacherous verbatim over the phone.

"So how's your writing coming along?" Rich asked, bringing Teflon back to the present.

"It's been a minute since you sent me something don't tell me you're slacking up in there," he joked.

"Never that," she replied back.

"I got something for you. You know I couldn't send you those last chapters," she added, referring to the intimate scenes she'd written about her and Treacherous.

"I understand. So when can I expect the new material? I started reading some of those street lit books just to compare to your work and you're just as good, if not better, than some of these authors out here," Rich complimented.

"Why you comparing me to them? I'm not trying to be no author. They ain't no different than rappers. Most of what they write either somebody told them or they was on the porch watching. They don't come from where we do. Seriously, I'm not impressed with that street lit shit," Teflon said.

"This story is for me, your grandson, and for you, nobody else. This is my life—our life. They talk it, we lived it," Teflon chimed.

"Relax, daughter-in-law," an understanding Rich replied. "No one's trying to turn you into an author. I was just letting you know how good I thought your work was," he added in attempts to calm Teflon. "You got skills that's all."

His reply had accomplished his intent.

"Thanks, ol' man," a more calm Teflon cooed, embracing Rich's compliment.

"And my bad," she then said.

"For what?"

"For basing at you."

"Is that what you were doing?" Rich made light of the situation.

"Not intentionally," Teflon answered.

"Sounded kinda soft to me."

"Whateva, ol' man. Ain't nuthin' soft about me. You're the one getting soft in your old age," she quickly shot back at Rich. The two of them both shared a laugh, and then a sudden silence filled the air.

"I miss him," Teflon said, breaking the silence.

"Me too, baby girl," Rich joined.

"Ha." she chuckled. "He used to call me that sometimes. You sounded just like him. And the funny thing is I never used to like it or that boo stuff, which he always called me, but I never told him that, I knew he meant it out of love but I just loved the way it sounded when he called me babe or just Tef. His voice was so raspy that when he called my name it sounded like he was calling me tough. Damn I miss his ass."

Her voice faded as her emotions began to well up. Rich smiled. He could hear the love in Teflon's tone as she spoke about his deceased son. The strength of their bond and love was obvious, even to a blind man. Whenever Teflon spoke of

Treacherous, just as he reminded her of his son, she reminded Rich of Teresa. "You sound like his mother sometimes to me." Rich stated. "Not your voice, but the love in it whenever you speak about my son. Teresa use to worship the ground I walked on and loved me more than the word itself. At first, I used to think it was because I had been there for her when she needed someone to be there the most, but it was more than that, it ran deeper. I never told you the story of how she and I had met. Hell, I never even told my son, but without going into depth over the phone, she had proven to be my rider from day one and 'til the day she breathed her last breath. All the way up until the day my son was born that's all she had ever been," Rich ended.

It was difficult to relive the past concerning Teresa. His only memories of a woman or love for that matter, aside from his time with Treacherous, were only of Teresa. Back then, he knew he was not in touch with his inner feelings nor was he an expressive man. It wasn't until he had gone to prison that he'd discovered how painful love could be and how he had deprived himself of the beauty and luxuries of it. Where he was once emotionless, while in prison his emotions enhanced, allowing him to feel for the first time. He couldn't help but to think about the time Treacherous had come to visit him for the first and ultimately the last time while he was in prison. It was because he had raised Treacherous to show no sign of emotions that when he himself showed them, his son had taken it as a sign of weakness, something that was foreign to him coming from his father and caused him to cut off all contact with him. That day Rich had never felt pain of that degree and capacity before he recalled it was a feeling that had haunted and continued to haunt him to this very day.

"Shit, look at us." Rich laughed, pulling himself back together after his emotional trip down memory lane.

"I know, right," Teflon agreed. "But we can't help who we love, though."

"I know that's right."

"Anyway, I finally found a lawyer to take your case," Rich changed the subject.

Teflon did not respond. Rich knew she had practically given up hope on coming home, but he was determined to try with all his being. He had seen some of the most airtight-seeming convictions get reversed, so he knew anything was possible when dealing with the judicial system.

"He said you have some good arguments," he continued. "I'll keep you posted."

"Have you found out anything about your grandson yet?" It was Teflon who now switched the subject.

"Still working on it," was all Rich offered.

"You have one minute remaining," the automated voice system interrupted.

"Okay. I'm gonna go, but I enjoyed talking to you as always, love is love," Teflon said, wrapping up their call.

Like always whenever he heard her speak the familiar words he grew silent. "Me too," he then replied, clearing his throat. "Make sure you send me those pages, I need something to read."

"I got you as soon as I reread it."

"Okay 'til the next hold ya head and stay a rider."

"Always, you too."

Chapter 15

"Breaking news, just in, police have arrested two Newport News men in connection to yet another bank robbery in the downtown area of Richmond after a gun battle erupted between five men and authorities. Two of the suspects were pronounced dead on the scene while police are in search of the fifth member of the attempted heist getaway, who sources are saying may have fled the scene of the crime with an estimated amount of a hundred-thousand dollars. The five men were believed to have retrieved over a half a million dollars during the robbery. Our sources also tell us that the suspects were ranging from ages of twenty-three to twenty-seven, heavily armed and dangerous. At least three of the men, including one of the deceased, had criminal records and the two captured and two deceased all bore gang-affiliated tattoos. Although police have not confirmed, sources are saying this may very well have been another case of an initiation into one of the surrounding gangs that continue to sweep the Virginia area."

"Little dumb asses." Rich shook his head in disgust as he watched the 32-inch television. Since he had been home not a day had gone by on the news that something about banks or gangs flashed across the screen. Ever since he had witnessed his son's demise on television while he was still incarcerated and because gangs didn't exist in his day, the reports left a bad taste in his mouth. Based on what Teflon had shared with him of her and his son's last caper, Rich believed that Treacherous had actually sat down and tried to plan a foolproof job despite the final outcome, but did not believe the recent bank robberies he heard about on the news had been thoroughly thought out. Rich felt himself to be one of Virginia's most notorious ex-robbers. He had caught some of the best of them slipping in the game and had pulled off some of VA's most talked-about and unsolved capers in history. Rich shook his head, grinned at the thought as he reflected back on one of his most infamous, and thought to be impossible heists in his robbery career that he knew he'd take to his grave.

***

Leslie Tyler, aka Big Les, cautiously turned onto the street he routinely turned onto every Thursday night, this time in his cram Mark V with the plush eggshell-white leather interior and whitewall tires to match. He owned a fleet of Caddies, from Fleetwoods to Devilles, compliments of the numbers and dope houses he had spread throughout the city of Portsmouth. Out of force of habit, he adjusted his rearview mirror as he checked to see if he was possibly being followed. This was what he was accustomed to doing ever since his spot on Harrison Street became his number-one cash cow–house. Being a naturally paranoid man himself, combined with the cocaine he snorted, Big Les was always careful when he was visiting the particular house. Each week for the past three months he made it a point to switch up the vehicles he used to pick up deliveries, taking back streets and circling the surrounding area three to four times before actually considering going to his moneymaking spot.

Convinced the coast was clear, Big Les cruised up the street toward the house. Once he had arrived, he pulled into the driveway of a beige and brown three-family house. To someone looking from the outside, one would assume that the home appeared to be a nice place to live, but behind closed doors, they could have never imagined another world existed. A world of negativity.

Big Les shut off the lights on the Mark V and continued to drive toward the back part of the house. He then killed the car's engine. Before exiting, he raised the medallion, which hung from his gold Italian link chain and twisted it slightly to the side, exposing the white powdered substance it possessed. Big Les then took his pinky fingernail and scooped the cocaine up. He sniffed half the powder up one nostril, then repeated the act with the other. Again, he checked his rearview mirror. Noticing he had white powder residue in the creases of his nostrils, Big Les wiped his nose with his fingers. The cocaine began to take an immediate effect on him. He wiped the residue from his fingers onto the gums of his mouth, instantly numbing them. He took a piece of spearmint out of the wrapper he had taken out of his inside blazer and popped it in his mouth. He then reached over to the glove compartment, unlocked it, and snatched up the .38 police special he concealed and shoved it into his belt. Looking around inside his car for nothing in particular, once he felt he had everything, Big Les opened the car door and got out. Normally when he visited the other houses, he'd conceal his weapon by buttoning his blazer, but in his main house recently Big Les had been keeping it out in the open as a form of intimidation toward his workers. They were pulling in too much money for him and instilling fear in them was the only way Big Les felt he could prevent any of them from crossing him or trying to rob him. The cocaine now in full effect, Big Les felt like King Kong ready to take on Godzilla.

He took one last look over in the reflection of the Mark V's window. He was a neat freak and the drug had him thinking that something was out of place. He began to brush himself off with his hands, starting with his shoulders, down to the legs of his pants. When he came back up, that's when he saw what was really out of place in the reflection of the car window. He wanted to react, but his reflexes failed him.

"Don't be stupid, hero," Rich warned him, disarming him of the pistol in his waistband.

"This is some kind of joke, right?" Big Les laughed.

"You're the only joke, Les," Rich retorted.

Hearing his name did something to Big Les. Between the cocaine in his system and his big ego he was not in the least bit afraid.

"Nigga, you know who I am and you still got the nerve to pull this shit. You must be suicidal."

"Whateva you say," Rich said before punching Big Les in the back with the pair of brass knuckles he had on his left hand.

Big Les went crashing to the ground on one knee. He looked up just in time to see the masked gunman delivering a blow with the brass knuckles aimed at his jawline. Rich heard the sounds of teeth cracking as the punch landed on the side of Big Les's face. Rich went to deliver another blow, only to be stopped by the wave of Big Les's hand.

"You got it my man. Whatever you want," he surrendered through a bloodied mouth. Big Les was leaking like a faucet. Rich knew he had broken the big man down.

"This is what I want you to do," Rich started out.

Once Rich filled Big Les in on what was expected of him he escorted him up to the stash house.

"Who?" Tiny asked, recognizing the secret knock.

"Who you?" was Big Les's response. This was the secret answer to the question he asked his workers. Under any other circumstances he would have made an attempt to alarm Tiny, who stood on the other side of the door with a doubled-barrel sawed-off shotgun, but he couldn't take the chance of getting hit in the process or furthermore being killed by the gunman standing on the side of him. Tiny began unlocking the four bolts on the stash house's steel door. When he opened it up he was met with a revolver pointed at his head. "Easy, big man, don't be a hero. It's not your money," Rich said in a low tone, disarming him of the sawed-off. He noticed how big the man was and knew he'd have to take his life fast if he even blinked too many times.

"Do as he says, Tiny," Big Les instructed. Tiny saw the damage done to Big Les's face and knew the man with the gun pointed at him meant business. He did as he was told. Rich couldn't help but laugh to himself at the big man's monarch. "Here, tie him up," Rich told Big Les, handing him the duct tape. "And cover his mouth too."

Once that was done Rich stuffed the big man into a corner out of plain view.

"Hey boss," the worker posted up by the door greeted. He didn't even notice the bruises on Big Les's face due to the dimness of the hallway.

"What's happenin' Major?"

He never got to answer nor did he see Rich come up from his blind side.

"I'ma tell you like I told ya boy Tiny, be easy and don't be a hero. It's not your money," Rich repeated, putting the barrel of his gun to the man's temple.

Without realizing it Major's beige Swedish knit pants became soiled with urine.

"You got it, blood." Major threw his hands up. Big Les couldn't believe he had such a coward in his camp.

"You know the drill," Rich said to Big Les. He performed the same treatment on Major that he had Tiny.

Once Rich secured Major he instructed Big Les to open the door. He had already given him the layout and what to expect on the other side and Rich was prepared. If anything looked any different than what was told to him, Rich had already made up his mind that Big Les would be the first to die. When the door opened all Big Les's workers were surprised to see him. They were even more surprised when they saw Rich appear. Some were off to the right playing a game of spades while exchanging sticks of weed and sipping on beer and liquor, while one man and two women, all three in the nude with face masks, were off to the left in the kitchen area bottling up product. Two men were sitting on an old sofa directly in front, counting stacks of money with two guns and a bunch of rubber bands on the table and duffel bags beside them. Before anyone had time to react Rich sprung into action.

"Everybody relax," he suggested, coming up behind Big Les with one revolver pointed at his head, the other scanning the area. Despite it seeming as if everyone in the room was going to comply, Rich knew there was going to be one who would rebel. Just as he figured, as soon as the insurgent emerged from the table in front of him and Big Les, Rich sent two convincers that tore into the man's chest plate, giving him two good reasons why his decision was a bad one. He never got to get off a shot. If anyone had it on their mind to buck, it was easily changed by their colleague's sudden death.

"Do anybody else need convincin' that this is not a drill, it's the real deal?" Rich asked.

He saw everyone's head shaking, indicating they understood.

"Everybody come where I can see you." Everyone made their way over to the middle of the room. "Have a seat," Rich pointed to the ground. He pushed Big Les into the middle of the floor. "Tie 'em all up and tape the mouths."

Big Les was growing tired of Rich ordering him around. Judging by the money on the table and what he estimated to be in the duffel bags, he knew he was about to take a huge loss. In addition to that, he knew once word got out on the streets that someone had single-handedly took down one of his stash houses it would be just a matter of time before every petty stickup kid in town would try him and he couldn't afford to let that happen. Big Les began duct-taping his workers' hands behind their backs, starting from the right side. As he got to the middle person who was one of the naked girls he had bottling up for him, Big Les made his move. He had no idea Rich had already anticipated his move, though. The shot shattered Big Les's spine as he reached for the gun on the coffee table. The table legs collapsed from the weight of Big Les's body as he bellied over onto it. The women screamed as the men's eyes widened with fear. With no more time to waste Rich walked over to each person on the floor and one by one began launching bullets into the skulls. He then pushed Big Les's body to the side, gathered up all the money on the table, tossed it into the duffel bags, and exited the dead body–infested room. He had no need for the drugs so he left it where it was. On his way out he pumped a shot into Major's head. Seeing that he only had one shot remaining, Rich picked up the sawed-off shotgun Tiny once possessed and split his face into two before he made his way out the door. That night Rich had gotten away with 160,000 in cash and even up until that day the incident sat in the cold-case files and among the street tales as one of the greatest unsolved mysteries in the hood.

Rich brought his mind back to the present just in time to see the mug shots of the captured young bank robbers and shook his head in disgust for a second time. "Amateurs," he said as he shut the television off and called it a night.

Chapter 16

One year later

"The following people have legal mail," the CO announced.

Teflon was listening to CNN through her Walkman with one earbud in her ear while the other dangled from her side when she heard the officer call her name. She wondered what type of legal mail she could possibly be receiving as she walked over to where the officer stood and waited in line. When she was handed the white envelope the first thing she glanced at was the return address that read *United States of America Appellate Court*. Already knowing procedures, Teflon opened the envelope, took out the letter without bothering to read it, unfolded it and shook it out. Once she signed for it she put the letter back into the envelope, folded it back up, shoved it into her khakis' pocket, and resumed watching the news. Two hours had

gone by before the floor officer called count time.
Teflon wasted no time making her way to her
sleeping quarters. In passing she crossed paths
with her unit manager. Over the years she and
the white lady had never seen eye to eye. Teflon
felt her unit manager was intimidated by her.
The two had never exchanged words, but what
little they had was enough to support Teflon's
claim. Teflon never broke the white lady's stare,
who was eyeing her down from the time the two
had noticed one another in the hallway as their
paths closed in. She knew her unit manager
was on her way home, because this was the
time she'd normally see her floating through
the halls headed toward the unit's exit. As they
reached within ear distance of each other Teflon
noticed her unit manager fixing her mouth
to say something and was surprised because
they never spoke in the halls or anywhere else
whenever they were in each other's company.
"Congratulations, I'll see you in the morning,"
she drily remarked and kept going about her
business.

Teflon had no clue as to what the unit manager was talking about. She chalked it up as
the white lady believing in what was called the
"they all looked alike" concept, confusing her
with someone else in the facility. When count
time cleared, as usual Teflon took her ritual

shower. When she returned to her area she took the belt out of her khakis along with everything out her pockets to change from her sweatpants into a fresh, crisp pair. As she was emptying her pockets she came across the legal mail she had received earlier in the day. She took the envelope, balled it up, and tossed it into the trash. Just as she was about to slip out of her sweats and into her khakis something drew her to the trash can. She took the envelope back out of the can and un-balled it. She didn't know what made her retrieve the letter, but she was curious as to what the contents consisted of. Teflon took the letter out the envelope, unfolded it, and began to read.

Dear Ms. Jackson,
After carefully reviewing the arguments and mitigating factors of your case it is in the Appellate Court of the United States Of America's decision to find the charges you were trialed and convicted on unwarranted and grant you immediate release.
Sincerely,
Senior Judge Of Appeals
James A. Andrews

Teflon reread the letter for a second time before her brain could comprehend the words on the paper. Her eyes wanted to believe it, but she felt they were being deceived. By the time she had read the letter for a third time the words from her unit manager had registered in her head and Teflon realized the white lady in fact had the right person.

So many thoughts raced through Teflon's mind. She could not believe that she had been given a second chance. That in mind, her thoughts directed themselves to Rich. She knew he was the only one who could make this possible. For years he had been promising her that he would get her home. She never wanted to entertain the statement nor did she believe him, but at that moment he had turned her into a believer. She tucked the letter and speedily dressed. She couldn't wait to make her way to the telephone to share the good news with the only person she could.

The next day Teflon signed her release papers and walked out the female federal prison with nothing but a boxful of letters that Rich had written to her and nearly 300 pages of the manuscript she had been working on, in a laundry bag tossed over her shoulder. Everything else she left in her locker and let all the women in her area know they could have what they pleased. She had no friends, so there was no one in particular to leave anything to. The night prior she had stayed up writing a new chapter of her story until she fell asleep. When she had spoken to Rich to share the letter with him he had already known she was coming home. He had filled her in on how the Muslim attorney he had hired by the name of Damani Ingram from out of Maryland contacted him the day before, informing him of the court's judgment. Rich told her how he was referred to him by the attorney Muhammad Bashir who was also Muslim and had handled O.G.'s will and power of attorney papers for him. Rich was the one who had told Teflon she'd be released the next day and he'd be out front waiting on her when the doors opened. As promised, when she walked out there he was.

There was no mistaking who he was when she first laid eyes on him, thought Teflon. With the exception of the age factor Treacherous was the splitting image of Rich. Even the way he was seated on the Harley-Davidson bike instantly reminded her of Treacherous. She remembered how he had shared with her how his father had a love and passion for motorcycles. She saw Rich raise up from off the bike as she made her way over to him.

"What's up, ol' man," she said with a smile.

She was met with a bear hug. "What's goin' on, daughter-in-law."

Teflon was caught by surprise by Rich's hug, but it was way needed. She hadn't been embraced in a long time and it felt good to genuinely be hugged by a loved one. She hugged him back. "Let's get the fuck outta here," she then said.

Rich released his hold. "My thoughts exactly," he replied.

"Let me drive," Teflon requested.

"It's been a long time, you sure?" Rich asked with a smile.

"Of course. Once a rider always a rider," she replied.

Rich extended his hand. "After you then."

Teflon passed him her bag and hopped on the Harley. She turned the key in the ignition, grabbed the clutch, and started the powerful machine. The bike roared like the king of the jungle. The sound was like music to her ears. "Come on, ol' man, watchu' waitin' for?" Teflon yelled over the bike as she revved the engine. Rich grinned and hopped on the back. Teflon came out of first gear as if she had just ridden yesterday and within seconds Danbury Female Federal Correctional Institution became a thing of the past.

Chapter 17

Rich guided Teflon to the back of the house. As soon as he'd gotten word that she was coming home Rich went out and gathered as much as he could to make the back part of the house as cozy and comfortable as possible for her. He purchased her a brand-new mahogany and gold queen-sized bedroom set, a twenty-seven inch flat screen, a DVD/CD stereo system, and air conditioner, all to be delivered. He then went to Bed Bath & Beyond and snatched up a comforter set, throw with curtains to match, and extra pillows. Once he purchased that he went over to Target and picked her up any and all products he thought a woman may need, such as bottles of Dove moisturizer soap, Secret deodorant, Curél lotion with shea butter, and Aveeno body scrub, Motions shampoo and conditioner, along with towels and washcloths. He felt kind of weird shopping for the items, especially when he caught occasional glances and looks from female shoppers, but he told himself it had to be done. He was tempted to grab the more personal products he thought she may need, but sided against after seeing the many women in the aisle where the products were held. He was even tempted to buy her female undergarments but had no idea as to the size she wore and thought it to be inappropriate. So instead he picked her up a pack of wife beaters and boxer briefs. Once he had everything inside the room he began to put it together as best he could. When Teflon walked through the door she was both surprised and impressed. She had no idea what to expect, but she never expected all of what she laid her eyes on. The room was immaculate, she thought. She could tell everything was brought brand new by the fresh smell of newness in the air. Rich had everything laid out nice and neat for her, Teflon noticed. She smiled when she saw the pack of wife beaters and boxer briefs lying on the bed next to the towel and washcloth. "How'd you know," she said, actually glad he had chosen them over traditional bra and panties for her.

He just grinned. "I'll leave you alone to get situated, hope I got you everything you needed."

"You did good," she said, touching his face.

"I'll be downstairs," he replied and with that Rich was out the door.

***

Teflon had been soaking for nearly an hour in the hot bath. The realization of being home had just begun to marinate as she felt the products Rich had brought for her cleansing her flesh. She stood and drained the tub and rinsed the remainder of the prison residue off her body. As the shower water cascaded down her back, she held her head underneath the water, placed her two fingers on her clit, and traveled back in time when Treacherous had first come home.

"Thanks for the meal, babe," Treacherous said to Teflon, reaching over to give her a kiss.

"You know you don't have to thank me. You're my heart. I just wanted everything to be nice for you," she replied, embracing him. "You're home now. This is just the beginning." She continued to wash the upper part of Treacherous's back. He relaxed in the bath she had prepared for him. He had been soaking for half an hour while Teflon bathed him. Teflon dipped the washcloth into the water, then squeezed it out over top of Treacherous's clean-shaven head. Treacherous's dome glistened as the suds washed away. Teflon massaged his pecs as she continued to wash the residue off him, causing it to cascade from his

head onto his chocolate chest, which was rock solid. Each part of his body she touched was hard and chiseled with muscles. That turned Teflon on.

"This shit feels good. I couldn't wait to get up outta there and get that jail funk off me. Babe, I ain't never going back. We ain't never going back, you hear me," Treacherous spat in disgust, turning toward Teflon.

"I know, baby, I hear you," Teflon agreed. She could hear the hostility in Treacherous's tone.

"Let's not dwell on that, Treach. Let's just focus on us and how we're going to get this money. Fuck all that other stuff. Remember. No looking back."

"Definitely, no looking back, hand me a towel. I'm done." Teflon reached over and retrieved the towel she had waiting for him. Treacherous stood and Teflon began to dry him. Treacherous's manhood grew as Teflon took him into her hand and began massaging it while drying him off.

"Chill," Treacherous moaned, unable to bear her touch.

"You chill," she shot back. "Let me do this." Teflon knew that his body was foreign to her touch and sensitive from being without a woman's physical touch.

Teflon took Treacherous by the hand and helped him out of the bathtub. Treacherous revealed a half smile. Treacherous could hear the sound of R&B music coming from the bedroom as he followed Teflon. The closer they got, the more the sounds of Color Me Badd's throwback "I Wanna Sex You Up" could be heard. As Teflon glided down the hallway Treacherous's sex began to stiffen even more. The sight of Teflon's firmness from behind simultaneously and rhythmically bouncing from up underneath the wife beater she wore and her hips swaying from side to side was turning him on. When Teflon opened the bedroom door, the first thing Treacherous noticed was the king-sized bed with satin sheets that were blue, his favorite color.

Teflon turned and kissed Treacherous lightly on his bare chest, then led him to the bed.

She sat at the edge of the bed and released the towel from around Treacherous's waist. He made an attempt to move in closer, but Teflon held him at bay, pressing her hands into his washboard midsection as he towered over her. Treacherous looked down at her. She could feel his eyes on her, but didn't return his stare. Instead, without hesitation she took Treacherous into her mouth. The warmth of Teflon's mouth *was indescribable. He had never felt the way he did at that very moment. Teflon gyrated her mouth back and forth on Treacherous's hardness. Having never performed fellatio before, a few times she gagged from the size of Treacherous's rock hardness. She could not even believe she was able to get so much as the head inside of her mouth, based on how Treacherous was packing. She grabbed hold of his waist for support. Even the side of his buttocks were sculpted and solid, she thought as she continued to sex Treacherous with her mouth.*

Treacherous continued to enjoy Teflon's performance. He had never experienced such a feeling before. As strong as he felt himself to be, Treacherous couldn't help but grab hold of Teflon's shoulders for balance. Each time he felt Teflon's lips reach midway on his dick his legs nearly gave way under him. A few times he heard her choke as she tried to take him into her mouth deeper. He knew he was well endowed, but regardless to the size of his manhood, he was convinced that all the working out he had ever done had not conditioned him for the workout Teflon was putting on him. He watched as Teflon's head now smoothly began to bob back and forth on his ten inches of chocolate. He could hear Teflon slurping over the music as she popped his sex in and out of her mouth. Teflon's performance put him in the state of mind of a suction cup the way her lips locked around him. Slowly but surely she was getting the hang of oral as she was eager to learn every inch of Treacherous's body tonight. Although she couldn't get into them, she had tried watching adult movies for pointers on how to please him and picked up on how to enhance the oral pleasure she was now displaying on him. He couldn't help but close his eyes and throw his head back, bracing himself with the help of her shoulders as Teflon vigorously attacked his sex. The more Teflon licked, sucked, and jerked, the more the feeling became unbearable for Treacherous, who tried everything in his power to withstand the enjoyment brought to him by Teflon, but he knew he had to bring the pleasurable feeling to an end before he exploded.

Treacherous lifted his head back up and opened his eyes. When he looked down for a second time he saw Teflon was staring up at him with him still in her mouth. Their eyes met. Fully turned on by the effect her mouth had on him, Teflon knew she was far from being a pro, still occasionally gagging and having to let up for air, but there was no doubt in her mind that Treacherous was enjoying every bit of it as she took all she could of him into her mouth. Treacherous couldn't help to look down and witness the love she was putting down on him. Their eyes met, as she too stared up at him she licked around his helmet. Neither of the two broke the stare. At that moment a connection was one that only the two of them would ever know. Teflon ran her tongue down the spine of Treacherous's rock-hard shaft. The volume of Treacherous's low moan increased at the feeling. She then took him back into her mouth, then out, and licked her way down, reaching his nut sack. That was all he could bear. Treacherous pulled back and pushed Teflon's head off him. Teflon shot him a devilish grin. She could tell by the way Treacherous's body slightly quivered that his sack was sensitive.

Teflon backed herself up onto the bed and parted her legs. "Come here," she called out to him childlike with a devilish grin plastered across her face as she extended her hands out. Treacherous leaned in to her embrace. He now had a clear view of Teflon's neatly shaven tunnel and her smooth inner thighs. For the first time, he noticed Teflon had a tribal tattoo on her waistline, which seemed to wrap around. This was something Teflon had never shared with him. He placed one hand around his dick. It was throbbing from the treatment it had just received from Teflon. She also reached out to Treacherous's manhood with one hand while touching herself with the other. She was on fire. Her love cave felt as if it were a volcano, dripping with lava. Teflon grabbed hold of Treacherous. At that moment all she wanted was to feel him inside of her. Only he and he alone could cool her cave with his hose. "Come here," she repeated. But Treacherous resisted. Instead, he reached out and pulled her toward him. Treacherous placed a light kiss on Teflon's forehead, then a hard one to her lips. Teflon accepted the kiss as it turned into a passionate one. The kiss seemed to last hours. It was Treacherous who broke the lip lock. Treacherous was now standing at the edge of the bed. He grabbed hold of Teflon's wife beater and lifted it over her head as she raised her arms. Teflon's vanilla-toned 36C's bounced out of the wife beater. Treacherous cupped them both and put them together. He kneeled and began to nurse Teflon's pink left nipple, then did the same to the right. Teflon moaned. Chills shot through her body as Treacherous' warm tongue tickled her nipples.

Treacherous took Teflon's right breast into his mouth. While he squeezed her right mound

*with his left hand and sucked the juice out it,
he massaged Teflon's love cave with the other.
Treacherous felt Teflon's wetness. She was dripping of her own sex. Her juices had overflowed
onto Treacherous's hand. He could feel Teflon's
hips rotating and grinding into his fingers. He
heard her mumble through her moans, but
couldn't make it out over the sounds of the music dominating the air. Treacherous continued
to travel downward, licking every inch and
crevice of Teflon's body.*

*"Oooh." Teflon sighed, arching her back as
Treacherous toyed with her navel with his
tongue. Chills continued to jolt through Teflon's
entire body from Treacherous's touch. She had
never been so turned on in her life. Treacherous
made his way between Teflon's inner thighs,
planting kisses and gentle bites between them.
Never being between a woman's thighs before,
Treacherous had no clue as to what he was
doing, but he knew he wanted to reciprocate the
love she had shown him. Each time Treacherous
pressed his teeth into Teflon's skin, she flinched.
No one had ever gone down on her before, so
she wasn't sure if he was doing it right, but
because it was Treacherous it felt right. She
shifted her hips as she moaned from the pleasure the bites brought to her body. She began*

to enjoy the way he dug into her flesh with his mouth. It was more sensual than painful. Treacherous tried his best to please Teflon. Her scent drew him in and made him want to taste her. She had a natural scent, thought Treacherous. As the side of his face continued to brush up against and rest on Teflon's sex, he was ready to explore her in that way with his mouth. He knew that Teflon's body was responsive to him, as his was to her. Treacherous slowly turned his head to meet Teflon's sex. Her natural sweet-smelling fragrance between her legs as he was now full faced with her sex. He placed his mouth just below where Teflon should have possessed a patch of hair. He gently bit into her clit. "No," he heard her moan with her hands locked on the sides of Treacherous's head. Teflon had been so caught up in Treacherous's lips and tongue on her body she hadn't noticed he had made his way to her pussy.

"What's wrong?"

"Nothing, I just don't want you to. I wanna feel you inside me." She knew she would be able to give but wasn't too thrilled about receiving. Though she never experienced sex before she knew she would be more of a flesh-on-flesh type of sister. "Come here," Teflon replied, pulling Treacherous toward. Teflon's words shot *straight to Treacherous's dick. His manhood stiffened more. Teflon parted her legs more and slid back onto the bed, then reached out and took hold of Treacherous's sex as he slid with her. Treacherous towered over her as Teflon tried to place the head of his hardness inside of her.*

She sighed. What she had never told Treacherous or anyone, for that matter, was she had never been with a man before.

"You okay?" Treacherous asked, concerned.

"Yeah, baby, I'm good," she said. "It's just that you're big and . . . I never been with anybody before."

Her words caught Treacherous off guard. They had touched on many topics in the detention center, personal and in depth, and Teflon had never revealed she was a virgin, even when he had disclosed his only sexual encounter. He knew that after tonight he and Teflon would learn everything there was to know about each other sexually and that no one would touch the other ever again.

"Don't worry, I got you," Treacherous told her. Treacherous leaned in and began kissing Teflon slowly and passionately taking hold of his manhood, rubbing it around Teflon's sex in a circular motion, then up and down, occa-

sionally placing the head inside of her. Teflon continued to moan. She could feel herself getting even wetter from Treacherous's foreplay. She began kissing him harder, then gasped.

"I got you," Treacherous assured her, lifting up his upper body. Treacherous slid half of himself inside of Teflon. Her wetness allowed him to enter her with ease. The pain was excruciating for Teflon, but pleasurable at the same time. She watched as Treacherous artistically got her sex to open up to him. Each time she tried to match his stroke her muscles tightened. The more Treacherous stroked the wetter Teflon became. Treacherous's strokes became deeper. He could feel himself all the way inside of her now and so could she. Tears trickled down the side of her face from the foreign pain, but she refused to tell Treacherous to stop. It felt as if he were splitting her in two. Treacherous laid his upper body onto Teflon as he continued pumping her insides. He could feel Teflon's juices all over him as her muscles clenched his. Treacherous cupped Teflon's butt cheeks and spread them apart. It felt as if he'd opened up a new door. Even Teflon felt the difference as she was now able to semi-match Treacherous's thrust. Treacherous slid his sex in and out of Teflon with ease. He could hear juices talking

between the two of them. Treacherous felt he was ready to try a different position. Just when he was about to pull out and turn her over, Teflon wrapped her legs around him and locked him in.

"Oh shit, oh shit," she repeated. "Shit, baby, I'm about to cum." She thrust her hips into Treacherous. It was Treacherous who now had to match Teflon. "Ooh, yeah baby," Teflon groaned.

That was all Treacherous could withstand. He felt himself building up inside. "Damn, damn," was all he could muster as he aggressively pumped his dick into Teflon.

"Yeah cum with me, baby," Teflon cooed, digging her nails into Treacherous's back.

"Agh, I'm cummin' babe, I'm cummin'" Treacherous growled, increasing his pace as Teflon's nails caused him to arch.

"Me too," Teflon announced, gyrating her hips into him. Together they battled for supremacy as their juices intertwined.

"That was good," an out-of-breath Teflon managed to say when they finished. "Definitely," was what she got in return from an equally out-of-breath Treacherous.

Treacherous rolled off Teflon and onto the left side of the bed. Teflon leaned over and *placed her head on Treacherous's rock-hard chest, throwing one of her legs over his. "I love you, Treach," she purred.*

"I love you too, babe."

Teflon was reaching her second consecutive multiple orgasm as she heard Treacherous's voice inside her head. Her clit was throbbing at the thought of their first sexual encounter with each other. As her juices came flowing down, tears began to well up in Teflon's eyes. So many emotions were intertwined within her final climax. She turned the shower off, stepped out the bathtub, and began to dry herself. She then made her way to the room and began opening the grooming products on the nightstand that Rich had brought. As she began to lotion her body she couldn't help but admire her own beauty. Her thought at that moment was that she wished Treacherous was there to enjoy it. Teflon squeezed her eyes tight, then opened them. She knew if she continued to carry on the way she was she'd drive herself mad. She knew there was only one thing that would offer her mind some type of relief. After she finished grooming, Teflon put in Biggie Smalls's *Greatest*

Hits CD Rich had among the selection of music for her and pulled out her pen and pad out of the laundry bag and laid across the bed and began to work on her book.

Chapter 18

"I'm sorry Ms. Jackson, this is policy. I'm only doing my job," the social worker said apologetically.

"I understand that, but why do I have to keep going through this?" she questioned, maintaining her composure. "I've filled out every piece of paper that you people asked me and I'm still getting the runaround."

"Again, I apologize, but I am only here today to monitor visitation, nothing more. I will say that these things take time, it's a process," she stated and then cleared her throat before she spoke her next words. "And no disrespect to you, but considering your history, social services is going to be going over all of your papers with a fine-tooth comb, dotting all i's and crossing all t's. That's just the way the system works."

It took all the strength she had not to reach over and grab the social worker by the throat and strangle the life out of her. She had no

idea what type of history she had, Teflon knew.
Had she, the social worker would've chosen her
words more carefully, she told herself. Teflon
had reached the point beyond frustration. She
had been home for ninety days now and since
then her focus had been getting her son. When
she first paid a visit to social services she was
bombarded with what seemed like a ton of
paperwork to fill out. Based on what little Rich
had found out while she was still in prison
and the caseworker she knew, Treacherous
was being bounced around from one group
home to another. It fumed her when she was
first refused to see him before being told the
requirements it took in order to be granted a
visit. Rather handling things the wrong way,
Teflon accepted the paper with the guidelines
that would enable her to see her son. She also
filled out and returned all forms to begin the
process of gaining custody over her child. Now
ninety days later she was sitting as patient as
one could in her position, waiting for someone
to bring Treacherous in. She was irritated by
the social worker's presence, but knew for now
this was the only way. In her best tone Teflon
asked, "Well, how long do you estimate it would
be before I'll know something?"

"Ms. Jackson, I really can't tell you that. I mean, it can be six months, a year or two. It's not my decision."

Teflon couldn't believe her ears. The social worker's words tore into her heart. She knew it would be a process, but she did not think it would be as long of a one as the social worker had just shared. She cursed the system for the way they handled things. From day one she felt the system had failed her and yet knowing that she still tried it their way. Now it was failing her again. "You're right, it's not your decision," Teflon replied in a flat tone.

Neither the social worker or Teflon spoke another word to the other. The tension thickened as the silence between the two continued. Five minutes later it began to clear as both Teflon and the social worker saw the two male figures approaching. Teflon stood up as her son grew close. The social worker also stood.

"Thank you, Sean. Hello, Treacherous." She nodded to the escort and extended her hand.

"Hi, Ms. Paterson." He shook her hand while eyeing the stranger standing next to her.

The male escort left the three of them alone.

"Do you know who this is?" the social worker asked him, seeing the expression on his face.

Treacherous shook his head no.

"I'm your—"

"Ms. Jackson, please," the social worker interjected.

Had she caught the look on Teflon's face after cutting her words short her heart may have stopped. The hairs on the back of Teflon's neck were at attention. She had killed people for less, but she knew she had to keep her cool for her son's sake, but she made a mental note to remember the day.

"This is your mom," the social worker said to Treacherous.

She might as well have spoken Chinese, because her words were foreign to him. No one had ever spoken about his parents to him, let alone a parent and he never asked. Treacherous wondered whether the social worker was trying to tell him he had been adopted by the woman in front of him or was this who he'd be staying with from now until whenever they decided to ship him off somewhere again. As he studied the woman he began to realize that this was not someone who was adopting him or a woman he'd be residing with temporarily. Her eyes were familiar to him. They resembled the ones he saw when he looked at himself in the mirror. Her grain of hair answered his question as to where he had gotten such a good texture and they shared the same nose. Treacherous could not believe his eyes. Although no one ever said it, he was under the assumption his parents were either dead or had abandoned him. He had often wondered who and what he had come from and now part of that question was answered.

Teflon could see the confused look on his face. It was a look she'd often seen on his father's face whenever he was in deep thought. There was no doubt about it: He was definitely her and Treacherous's child. She fought back her tears as she saw the two of them in her son. She did not imagine she would be so emotional once she'd actually laid eyes on Treacherous junior. At that moment all Teflon wanted to do was snatch her son up and take him home with her.

"Hey man," she spoke.

"Hi," he replied, childlike. His eyes widened and he bit into his bottom lip the way Teflon knew she sometimes did when she was his age when she was trying to collect her thoughts.

"Treacherous, you do understand that no one's forcing you to be here. You don't have to if you don't want to," the social worker interjected, doing her job. Teflon took it another way. She had enough of the social worker. Her patience with the lady had worn thin and refused to let the statement slide. "Bitch, that's your last time cuttin' me off," she blew up. "Your ass don't have to be here either, for the rest of your life," she threatened.

Treacherous was clueless. He had no idea what had just happened.

Unbeknown to Teflon, the social worker had hit the silent-alarm button on her walkie-talkie and within seconds two security guards came storming in along with the male escort who had ushered Treacherous into the room.

"Is there a problem, Ms. Paterson?" one of the security guards asked.

"Yes, Ms. Jackson was just leaving and I need for Mr. Freeman to be escorted back to his living quarters," she calmly stated. She knew she could have had Teflon arrested and charged for terroristic threats, but she chose not to. Although she didn't agree with her, she understood her position as a mother and didn't want to create any more problems or headache than she already had between her past and trying to gain custody of her son. Based on her behavior, she intended to report she knew the state would never award her custody of the child, no time soon anyway, she was sure of.

Teflon was fighting with the decision to black out and jump on the social worker, but thought better of it knowing the ending result. She couldn't believe she had just snapped the way she had, but the social worker had pushed one too many of her buttons. She knew the lady could have taken things to the next level and made matters worse, but Teflon was not appreciative at all toward her making light of the situation. She was flaming inside and knew someone would pay dearly for how she felt.

"Come on Treacherous," the escort said, putting his arm around him.

"Bye Mom," he said, waving. His words were like a fist that had just squeezed all the life out of Teflon's heart. Before she could respond Treacherous was whisked out the room.

"Ma'am," one of the security guards reached.

"Don't fuckin' touch me," Teflon roared. She snatched away from the man and made her way to the door.

Rich was parked alongside Teflon's bike when she came out of the state building. He could see by the look on her face something was wrong. By the time she reached him she had just wiped her last tear.

"What's going on?" he asked.

"These muthafuckas playing games," she shouted.

"Whoa, what happened?"

"They don't wanna give me my fuckin' son, that's what happened."

Her voice echoed in the air as her words boomed out her mouth. Rich was hoping that wasn't the case, but had expected as much. When he'd first come home, aside from keeping track of where his grandson was being shipped to every time they transferred him, Rich had also run into a dead end and brick wall trying to find the best way to gain custody of Treacherous. Many times he was tempted to take a different route in getting his grandson, but sided against it, thinking Teflon would be able to come home and have a better chance. He realized he was wrong. He was now glad he had stuck with what he had been looking into for the past eight months figuring he might need it for a rainy day. A thunderstorm had just hit their family and he knew that day had now come.

"What did they say?" he wanted to know.

"Fuck what they said. I want my son and if they don't give him to me I'ma fuckin' take him."

Rich let her words resonate. Before he said anything he first wanted to be clear on whether Teflon had meant what she had just said.

"Are you sure that's what you want?"

"Rich, please don't start preachin' and shit to me. I want my fuckin' son and I'ma get 'em by any means," she spit.

"I'm not gonna preach to you. Let's go home. We got a lot of talking to do."

Teflon stared at him oddly. She couldn't help but notice the same look in Rich's face and tone of voice that his son had used the day he had filled her in on his thoughts that had changed their lives forever. She didn't say anything. Instead she climbed on her R1 as Rich started his Harley. The two of them backed out and peeled off. The whole ride home Teflon couldn't help but wonder had she been right about what she had picked up on.

That night the two of them talked until the sun came up. That very same night Rich confirmed her thoughts, allowing her to make them become her own and for the next few weeks the two of them went over Rich's plan until they ate, slept, and breathed it.

Chapter 19

"I'm tellin' you Troy don't count my Cowboys out this season. Jerry Jones is gonna build Dallas back up the way we were in the nineties. I mean, come on, you know football. Romo got Terrell Owens and Witten out there, not to mention Adam 'Pacman' Jones alongside with Terence Newman. And let's not forget Tank Johnson to clog the middle and stop the run. Hell, come to think of it, we may be better or just as good as the Troy Aikman, Michael Irvin, Emmitt Smith days," Gus continued. "You remember. When we spanked you guys," Gus ended with a chuckle. This was a ritual for him and Troy. Today it was football, other days it was baseball or basketball. The two had been partners for nearly four years and were as different as night and day. Gus was a forty-eight-year-old six feet two, 230- pound half Irish, half Italian ex- marine who loved rock and roll, fast cars, fast bikes, and fast women, not to mention a love for draft beer and even more for Cuban cigars. Troy, on the other hand, was a thirty-four-year-old African American nondrinking, nonsmoking grad of Hampton University. He was originally from Long Island, New York, but moved to Virginia his first year in college seventeen years prior. Standing five feet eight, weighing an even 210 pounds, rock solid, compliments of his dedication to the gym and past boxing training, light skin with light brown eyes to match and natural wavy hair, he would have appeared to be the ladies' man–type, but he was actually a one-woman man. He had been dating the same female since his freshman year in college, had been engaged for the past six months, and just added a new addition to their lives a month ago. It was his dream to become a homicide detective or crime scene investigator, but somehow settled for an armed security position. When he and Gus met, despite being opposites, the two hit it off immediately due to their common interest in sports.

"G, why do you continue to live in the past?" Troy returned with a chuckle of his own. "Everybody knows that the New York Giants pound for pound are the best team not only in the NFC but in the NFL."

"*Bullshit,*" Gus spit out through the phony cough in a humorous manner as he covered his mouth. "Back at you, if you think the Cowboys are," Troy retorted.

"I never said that, my friend, but we're definitely one of them. The proof is in the pudding. Five rings, young man. How many do you guys have?" Gus questioned, already knowing the answer. "You give your New York Midgets too much credit, but it's understandable, that's how you Northerners are, cocky sums'abitches."

"That's right, and we got three," Troy said, proud to be from New York and a New York Giants fan.

"My point exactly. And just know, we're in a much better position to get our sixth ring before you bums get your fourth."

"Whatever," was Troy's response. He reached for the volume of the truck's radio to increase the song's sound.

"Oh no you don't, it's my turn to pick the next song," Gus announced, reaching to change the radio station.

"Come on, Gus, this is my jam, after this one I promise I'll listen to whatever you want for the rest of the day."

Music was another topic the two debated over throughout their four years as partners and friends. They had been on the road since 6:00 a.m., alternating their preference of music back and forth. It was now a approaching 7:00 a.m. and they were due to arrive at their destination by 8:00 a.m. and nothing would make Gus happier then to be in control of the radio for the remainder of their journey to and fro. "Troy, you know all this hippitee-be-bop gives me a headache, but I tolerate it," Gus replied. To those who didn't know him one would take Gus's comments offensive, but Troy knew the older man meant know harm or disrespect.

"I know, but just this last one, besides, your music could cause me my job putting me to sleep." The two shared a laugh.

"Just this last one for the entire day, right?"

"Scout's honor."

"Fine."

"Thanks, friend."

Troy nodded his head and recited some of the verses to the hip-hop artist Jadakiss's song playing on the radio as Gus made his way down Highway 264 west.

"Man, check out that babe right there," Gus whistled as the motorcycle breezed past the truck.

"G, you know I only have eyes for my fiancée," Troy shot back, noticing the bike was occupied by a woman, judging by the figure.

"Not the babe on the bike, knucklehead, I'm talking about the bike, she's a beaut," Gus clarified, admiring the machine the female was riding.

"I knew that, just messing with you," Troy said, hoping Gus hadn't caught his embarrassment for thinking the obvious. He knew how much Gus loved motorcycles.

"She's riding that son of a gun. That's one of those R-ones right there. A lot of power in that sucker, kiddo. And see those chrome pipes, the best money can buy. She could come through an area and make that bike roar like the king of the jungle, doing about a hundred with ease right now."

"Is it faster than your Harley?" Troy asked, already knowing the answer, but wanting to show interest in his partner's love for bikes.

"Not in this lifetime."

Troy smiled.

Just then another bike blew past Gus and Troy on the right shoulder, passing both them and eventually the female.

"Now that's what I'm talking about," Gus roared.

"And that, my young friend, is what I'm talking about. That's a Boss Hog right there, my kind of bike, music to my ears." Gus gloated at the sight of the Harley-Davidson motorcycle that was no longer in eye distance.

"Look at them go," he continued to admire as the motorcycles both had now vanished up the interstate.

Ten minutes had gone by before Gus noticed the back of the female motorcycle in view up ahead, but the Harley was nowhere to be found. He knew she had to have made a pit stop if he was able to catch up to the powerful bike.

"There goes your baby again," joked Troy, noticing the same. They were just a few miles away from their intended exit before Troy dozed off. As the miles closed in so did they on the motorcycle.

"A nice morning like this and all of this open road. If I were her I'd be opening that bad boy up," Gus commented to no one in particular on the fact the bike was just cruising.

"Here we are," he then said to himself since Troy was sound asleep, seeing the exit ahead now only a thousand feet or so away from the bike that was to the left of them. The right-turn signal of the motorcycle lit up and Gus instantly caught it. Being a fellow rider himself, he slowed for the bike to cross over, seeing they were getting off on the same exit, but apparently the female rider hadn't noticed. She continued

to ride in the left lane as they approached the
exit. After the failed attempt Gus accelerated as
he began to get off the exit. The bike made an
attempt to exit also after nearly missing the turn
simultaneously to Gus exiting.

"Holy shit!" Gus shouted as the unexpected
happened.

Teflon could not have timed and executed her
next move any more perfectly then she had. She
and Rich had gone over this countless times.
She could see the driver of the truck courteously
signaling for her to exit before them. She intentionally disregarded his gesture. Seeing that he
had given up, Teflon watched as he sped up to
get out of her way so she too could exit. She too
sped up, hooking a sharp right, just inches from
missing the turn. Had she not gunned it as much
as she had the truck would have knocked her
into the right divider, but Gus was an excellent
driver and was able to come to a screeching
halt. The first thing he saw when he stopped was
Teflon losing control of the motorcycle and going
down on the exit ramp.

"What in the hell?" Troy questioned, waking
out of his slight stupor compliments of Gus's
choice of music.

"The crazy broad on the bike almost missed
the exit and tried to make it," shouted Gus, already unfastening his seat belt.

"No, I'll go and check on her, you call it in," Troy suggested, unhooking his seat belt, as well as reaching for his issued weapon out of the glove compartment.

"Just stay here, I got it," Gus insisted, hand already on the handle of the driver's door.

"Okay, you want me to call it in?"

"Hold off, we may need to call an ambulance first if she's hurt, or she may just have the wind knocked out of her. Believe me, I know," he said as he hopped out of the truck. Against his better judgment Troy rolled with his partner. Gus made a beeline over to where the fallen female lay. It dawned on him that he had left his weapon back in the truck. His first thought was to double back and retrieve it, but shook off the notion as he was just feet away from the female and bike. Troy watched attentively as his partner made his way to the motorcycle.

Teflon could hear the heels of the truck driver's click- clacking on the pavement as he approached her.

"Ma'am?" His voice let her know he was close by.

"Ma'am can you hear me?" Gus kneeled down.

"Ma'am can you—" Gus attempted to repeat only to have his next words cut short.

The three shots in succession from the silencer weapon pierced his flesh and lodged into his lower abdomen just under his bulletproof vest. Gus never had time to think or had a chance to regret stepping out of the armored truck to aid the female without his weapon as a fourth shot followed, ripping into his skull as death greeted him. Troy sat impatiently, glancing at his watch, wondering what was taking his partner so long. They were indeed behind schedule and that was unlike his partner. Something wasn't right, thought Troy. He could feel it. Unable to wait any longer, Troy honked the horn. Already they were in violation according to policy by stopping. On top of that they hadn't called the stop in. Noticing that Gus continued to kneel hovered over the female rider and not responsive to the sound of the horn, Troy opened the passenger door and stood out onto the running board. He was so focused on Gus that he had no way of knowing what awaited him outside the armored truck door. Had he just taken a second to scan and secure the area the outcome of what was about to transpire may have been different.

"Gus," he called out. "Gus—aagh!"

Like Teflon, Rich carried out his part of the plan to a T. It couldn't have gone any better than he had envisioned it in his mind a thousand

times so far. He had done his homework on
the white security guard enough to know that
Teflon's seeming accident would cause his plan
to unfold the way it was now. What little he had
found out about the younger of the duo was
enough to convince Rich that he was the least
of a factor. Even now, seeing his carelessness
by opening the armored truck's door was only
confirmation in Rich's eyes that the caper would
go as smooth as he intended. Teflon's diversion
had done the trick, thought Rich, as he crept up
from the side and scaled the armored truck. Just
as the door opened Rich partially saw the black
security guard's body exposed and immediately
sprang into action. The penetration and heat
of the first shot of one of Rich's infamous .38
revolvers caused Troy to scream out in agony
as it shattered his hip bone, causing him to lose
balance in the doorway of the armored truck.
As Troy fell onto the highway's pavement, Rich
hovered over him. At the sound of Rich's weapon,
Teflon released her hold of the white security
guard, who she had been firmly holding onto
to prevent him from falling back and alarming
his partner of danger. She was grateful for all
the working-out she had done while in prison,
for had it not been for the physical strength she
had built while incarcerated she didn't think

she would have been able to hold him as long as she had. She then slid herself from under her bike, raised up, lifted her motorcycle onto its kickstand, and stepped over the lifeless body. As an extra precaution and confirmation, Teflon dumped two more slugs into the slain security guard's melon before locating and retrieving the keys to the armored truck, then made her way over to the vehicle. She checked her watch, which was synchronized with Rich's and running on stopwatch time. They were right on schedule according to the time that had elapsed since her staged fall.

Troy lay there helplessly wondering what had just happened. Furthermore, where was his partner? All types of thoughts were racing through Troy's mind as tears poured out of his eyes, soiling his face. Each time he tried to open his eyes he was met with a blur. All he could see was his life flashing before his very own eyes and thought to himself this was not the way he wanted to die. His thoughts were interrupted by the sound of voices. "We need to get a move on things," Teflon stated. Despite for the most part being calm she couldn't help but to be somewhat antsy. Not out of fear, but out of familiarity. Since Rich had laid down what they had to do and what was expected of her, it had Teflon revisiting the last time she had to ride for a man she had loved and would lay her life on the line for in such capacity. Never in a million years would she have thought she would find herself in a similar type of predicament that had cost her her freedom and the one man she ever truly loved. The ride or die chick in her convinced Teflon that this time was different, gonna be different, for a different cause.

"Absolutely," Rich agreed. "Soon as I finish this," he added, pointing his guns at the security guard's body. Hearing those words sent an indescribable feeling throughout Troy's entire body. It was evident to him now that the female rider was a part of the setup, just as it was apparent that his partner was dead. As if on cue his eyes popped opened and his vision became clear as his survival instincts kicked in. The first thing he saw was Rich towering over him with two revolvers in hand pointed at him. "Please man, don't kill me!" screamed Troy, raising his hands up as if they would be able to prevent shots they might be intended for his face. "Please, I'm begging you," he continued. "I have a family. A wife and little boy," he offered for sympathy. His words were disregarded, though.

"You should've thought about that before you chose this profession, youngin,'" was Rich's response as he raised his two revolvers and emptied them into the upper and lower parts of the security guard. Slugs riddled Troy's body.

Not wasting any more time, Rich checked his watch and made his way to the back of the armored truck.

By the time he reached the back Teflon had already transferred a great deal of cash from two of the money bags into her duffel bag and was working on a third one.

"Only take as much as you can handle," suggested Rich.

Teflon paused and looked back at him. For a minute she thought she was looking at Treacherous, the resemblance now more stronger then ever and there was no doubt in her mind that his words would have and could have come out of his son's own mouth had he been the one she was doing the job with.

"Relax. You keep forgetting, ol' man, that you're not the only one who worked out in the joint. Take your own advice and try not to hurt your back," she told Rich as she continued to stuff her bag with monies. Now was not the time for back-and-forth, Rich knew. He shook his head, chuckled, and made a mental note to finish at a later date when this was all over with. After all, this was what their relationship had been built on. Rich dove right in, pulling his duffel bag out and began following suit. Teflon glanced at her watch once again. "We gotta go," she informed Rich. "The clock is ticking."

Rich looked at his own watch. In total, sixteen minutes and twenty-two seconds had gone by. They were still eight minutes and thirty-eight seconds ahead of schedule. Although he was fully prepared, Rich was grateful no other vehicles had attempted to exit the ramp. He didn't want any more casualties than there had to be, but no one was exempt, he reasoned, if they walked into the line of fire.

"Okay, you go ahead, I'll meet you," he told her.

"See you there." Teflon slid the duffel bag full of money to the edge of the armored, truck then hopped out and turned facing backwards. Once she had the bags strapped over her shoulders she made her way to her R1. Rich hurried to fill his duffel bag, zipped it up, then did as Teflon had with hers. *So far, so good,* he thought, commending himself for putting together and executing such a foolproof plan. As he walked from around the armored truck intending to head for his Harley, he saw Teflon straddling her bike. Satisfied that she was safe, Rich began to head for his own bike but something stopped

him in his tracks. Something he never anticipated.

As Teflon started her motorcycle she thought
she'd heard something other then the bike's
engine and swung around to see what the sudden noise had been. Reflexively, upon turning
around her question was answered as she locked
in on the unthinkable. "Rich!" she cried as she
snatched off her helmet, slithered her arms out
of the duffel bag's straps in lightning speed and
drew her weapon.

Rich never saw the bullet coming that had
ripped through the left side of his neck and
traveled downward, finding a resting place
right above his heart. The impact of the shot
slightly spun him around and planted him up
against the armored truck. More surprised then
anything, his eyes were opened wide enough
to see the second shot spiraling in midair toward his direction. He neither had the time or
the strength to reach for his AR-15, which was
strapped across his chest. His mind and body
fought for supremacy as one alerted him of the
danger approaching, advising him to stand
clear while the other resisted, keeping him at a
standstill. As the second shot plunged into his
upper torso, Rich could hear Teflon's cries in the
distance. He knew it was just a matter of time

before she made her way over to him. He was actually more concerned with her well-being then
he was with his own at that moment. The last
thing he wanted to see was their plans go in vain.
He couldn't believe he had been caught slipping
the way he had been. There was no doubt in his
mind that his final fate would be handed down
to him on the exit of the interstate. He had told
himself when he was released from prison that
returning was not an option. Rich never thought
this would be the way he breathed his last breath
on earth, but this was the life he had chosen for
himself, he knew, and he was content with what
came behind it. He and his shooter made eye
contact just before the third bullet was released.
The shooter's face was bloodied and unrecog-
nizable from the previous shots he had endured.
Rich couldn't help but respect the man's will to
live and serve out his duty, but didn't regret what
he had done to him. The only regret Rich had
was that he hadn't finished the security guard
off. Rich could hear the sounds of other shots in
the distance and knew the only place they could
be coming from.

Troy's head was spinning. He had just regained consciousness as he lay there fighting for
his life. Images of his fiancée and son paraded
in his mind. It was those images that kept him

holding on. Troy had felt each bullet pierce his flesh and knew he had been hit numerous times by the revolvers the robber unloaded in him, so he wasn't sure if he would make it. All he could think about was staying alive long enough for him to see his family one more time. Despite his body being filled with at least a half-dozen slugs, Troy felt a discomfort on his right side. Something was poking him and he knew what that something was. Troy strained to shift his body and lift his left arm to retrieve the weapon from underneath him. He remembered how he had placed it on his hip when he and Gus had stopped for the female's fake fall. He somehow managed to get his body to slightly shift just enough to reach his service weapon, but the weight of his arm felt like a ton each time he tried to raise it. Tears trickled out the corners of his eyes from the excruciating pain he was enduring, but still he refused to give up. He attempted to raise his arm for the fifth time. A sharp pain jolted his body as he raised it again just below his side. It seemed to be getting heavier and heavier with each strain. "No," Troy growled as he exerted all the strength he had into the attempt. It was enough to get his arm onto his chest. Accomplishing that, an out-of-breath Troy inched his hand toward the weapon.

A sense of achievement mixed with relief filled his body as he felt his fingertips brush the butt of his weapon. Having his left arm over his chest made it easier for Troy to shift his body now even more. He knew his next move was going to be crucial and had to be precise. All in one motion, Troy threw all his weight to his right side and slid his hand onto his weapon. As he felt himself rolling over, he was able to lock in on the weapon and pull it out before he landed on his stomach. Still out of breath, Troy let out a few blood-filled coughs. Just then he heard sounds coming from the back of the armored truck. He hoped the perpetrators hadn't heard him. Troy's adrenaline was pumping. With what little strength he still possessed Troy was able to release his safety on his .40 cal and aimed it in front of him, prepared for whoever or whatever came from behind the armored truck. Seconds turned into minutes without anyone coming from behind the vehicle, but Troy continued to play possum, laying there waiting patiently on the ground for any opportunity that might present itself. Just then Troy heard footsteps and knew it was either now or never. He focused his aim on the end of the armored truck and locked in. He knew he'd have to act fast and make his shots count. With each footstep Troy's heart rate increased, but no one appeared around the corner. The sound of the motorcycle's engine behind him startled Troy, nearly causing his heart to leap out his chest, but not enough to cause him to lose focus on his aim. Fortunately for Troy, he was able to maintain his composure. He would have never seen the robber before the robber had seen him as he came from around the side of the armored truck. Troy's right bloodstained eye grew small as it locked in on its intended target and without hesitation he fired a round. By the way the robber's body slammed up against the vehicle Troy knew his shot was successful. His second round was fired with confidence, finding its intended target once more. Troy's eyes met with the man who was responsible for him laying there on the ground. Although his seemed much darker and cold to him, Troy could see pain in his assailant's eyes and wondered had the man seen that same pain in his own eyes. If he had, he didn't care, Troy knew. He didn't care that he was another black man like himself and didn't care that he had a fiancée and kid waiting for him at home. And with that thought in mind Troy squeezed the trigger and released a third shot, but never got to see its final destination. The last thing Troy heard was a woman's voice.

Teflon was now off her bike with gun in hand racing toward the direction of where the sudden commotion erupted. The first thing she spotted was Rich planted up against the side of the armored truck. Instantly, she flew into a blind rage. She had just reached the security guard laid on the ground as he fired his next shot.

"Muthafucka!" Teflon screamed and without thinking twice she pumped three shots into the back of his head. She then rushed over to Rich.

Rich watched in admiration as Teflon finished off the security guard and came to his aid. If he ever had any doubt, which he hadn't, there was no room for any now as to why his son had loved her so much, thought Rich. At that moment Rich deemed Teflon the true definition of a ride or die chick.

"Shit," Teflon cursed, seeing the blood seeping out the side of Rich's neck. "Give me your hand." She placed Rich's hand on the side of his neck and pressed it against it. "Just hold that right there 'til I find something," she began, examining Rich's body for other wounds. "Where else are you hit?"

In attempts to make light of the situation, Rich cracked a smile. "Don't worry about me, baby girl. I'll be all right. You need to get out of here," he said calmly.

"What?"

"You heard me, you gotta go. You gotta stick to the plan."

"I see these fuckin' bullets got you delirious," Teflon said, ignoring his suggestion. "If you gonna talk stupid don't talk at all, save your strength," she added.

"Hold on youngin', I'm still your elder," Rich shot back.

"And you're also my partner, so act like it," Teflon shot right back. "We in this together, ride or die, right?"

Rich could not dispute that. That was the creed they lived by. "He caught me under here," he offered, indicating he had been hit in the upper torso.

"I gotta get you outta here." Teflon knew the only way Rich could have any chance of living was if she got him somewhere where she could nurse and dress his wounds. She also knew that she could not handle the one duffel bag, let alone two and Rich all on her bike. Her mind was operating at 200 miles per hour trying to figure out the best way to handle the situation. Just then an answer appeared.

A tired Judy Smith had been driving since 4:00 a.m. for the past three and half hours from

Washington, D.C. and was relieved to see that her exit was up ahead. Although she was tired, she was not in the least bit complaining. After all, this was the opportunity she had been waiting for. Being a thirty-two-year-old white female who had been working in corporations run by men since she was the ripe age of twenty-one, she jumped at the chance to represent the firm and be privy to the next promotional spot due to open. Her navigation system in the rental the company she worked for provided for her said she was only eight miles away from her final destination. Her business meeting was scheduled for 9:30, which gave her more then enough time to check into the hotel and make it to her meeting on time. *"In three hundred feet exit right,"* the navigation system announced. Judy put her turn signal on and veered over toward the exit.

"Fuck," she cursed under her breath, seeing that traffic was backed up on her exit. She slowed the Dodge Avenger down twenty feet from the back of the armored truck.

Judy impatiently checked her Rolex watch. "Come on, people," she yelled to no one in particular. Just then a woman appeared from the side of the armored truck heading in Judy's direction. There was no doubt in her mind now that an accident had occurred up ahead. Judy rolled down her driver's-side window to find out what was going on.

"Good morning."

That was all she was able to get out before Teflon drew her gun from behind her back and in one motion shoving the 9 mm in the car and dumping one shot in her skull. Part of Judy's brain matter splashed across the passenger's window as she slumped over the steering wheel. Teflon immediately sprung into action. She opened the driver's-side door and unfastened the seat belt, then grabbed the Caucasian woman by the back of the neck, snatched her up, and flung her out of the car. She checked the time on her watch. They were twelve minutes behind schedule with eighteen minutes remaining before the armored truck's drop-off would become suspicious and investigate. Teflon dragged the 103-pound white lady's body to the armored truck, reopened the back, picked her up, and tossed her inside.

"You still with me?" she asked Rich, who had now slid down to the ground.

"Yeah, barely," was his response.

"What's important is that you're still here. We don't have much time, I found us a way outta here," Teflon informed Rich.

"Yeah, I heard," he said, grinning in reference to the shot he'd heard moments ago.

"By any means necessary, right," Teflon stated.

"By any means necessary," he repeated.

"I need you to lift up so I can take this bag to the car," she then told Rich, leaning over him. Once she assisted Rich in freeing his arms from the duffel bag Teflon hiked the bag over her shoulder and lugged it to the car. She reached inside the Dodge Avenger and popped the trunk, then threw the duffel bag inside, then made her way to retrieve the one she had laid beside her bike. Once both bags were secured Teflon hurried back over to Rich.

"Come on ol' man, let's get you outta here," Teflon said as she reached down to help Rich from the ground.

"What I tell you about all of that old man non-sense. Ain't nothing ol' about me but my soul."

"Yeah yeah, you can tell me all about it later. Right now let me get you to this car," Teflon told him.

Rich noticed the unlucky person's brain matter plastered all over the passenger-side window as soon as Teflon opened the door.

"You gotta wipe that off before we go, can't be riding around like this," Rich advised right before she secured him in the car.

"I know."

Teflon took off her black-leather riding jacket then lifted her black *I Ride Hard* T-shirt off and began wiping the window. Satisfied she had gotten the bulk of the brain debris off she balled the T-shirt up. "Here, put this on your neck." She then threw her jacket inside the car, closed the door, and made her way to the driver's side.

She started the car and again took a look at her watch. Three seconds after she looked at the watch the alarm sounded on both hers and Rich's, indicating they had reached the time they had given themselves for the caper they had just pulled. They were supposed to have been long gone, but the unexpected had happened, just as it had when she and Treacherous had pulled their last caper together. Too many similarities, thought Teflon, but she refused to let the final outcome end the same. She threw the Avenger in reverse, and backed up off the ramp, then back onto the highway. She knew there was no way for authorities to trace the motorcycles back to them because they were stolen, so she had no problem leaving them on the exit ramp. Teflon put the car in drive and accelerated onto the highway headed for the next exit. Just as she sped off a car was slowing to exit. She counted her blessings for making it off the ramp in time and onto the highway unnoticed.

"Recalculating," the navigation system wailed out of nowhere. Teflon took the butt of her weapon and smashed the system until it went silent.

"You killing up everything today, huh?" Rich said humorously in a raspy tone, still applying pressure to his gunshot wound.

"I swear you and your son should have been twins," she laughed.

"No, you and him should have been brother and sister." The two of them both shared a laugh.

In record-breaking time, Teflon closed in on the exit, which was 7 miles from where they had just departed.

"I'm gonna stop and take care of you, then come back as soon as I get li'l Treach," Teflon suggested.

"Like hell you will," Rich sided against. "I'm good. Remember, we're in this together, ride or die."

"But—"

"But nothing. Let's stick to the script and go get my grandson," Rich took charge despite his condition. Teflon didn't argue with him. Instead, she exited off the highway and headed for the next destination.

Chapter 20

"Charlie one this is Charlie two," the helicopter radioed in.

"Go ahead Charlie two."

"I have visual on that location."

"Copy that Charlie two. What's the status?"

"We got two bodies, an armored car, two motorcycles, another vehicle, and a pedestrian on foot on exit eighty-seven on Interstate two-sixty-four. Requesting all available units to location."

"Copy that Charlie two."

The helicopter watched as the pedestrian continued to jump up and down, waving his arms in the air in attempts to flag him down. Unable to land and assist in whatever had taken place on the ramp, the helicopter hovered over the area until backup arrived on the scene. Within minutes all available units swarmed the surrounding area.

"Jesus freakin' Christ, what took you guys so freakin' long," the twenty-six-year-old Caucasian man named Todd ranted to the first officer to arrive, walking toward the patrol car as soon as the officer stepped out. "There's freakin' bodies all over the place."

Instantly he was met with a gun pointed in his direction. "Sir, stay where you, and let me see your hands," the trooper shouted.

"Holy shit," Todd nervously yelled, complying with the orders given to him. "Dude, you got the wrong guy," he managed to say.

"On your knees now," another trooper yelled his way with gun drawn as well.

"This is bullshit," Todd bellowed. "I called you fuckin' guys," he added, dropping to his knees. In seconds, Todd was surrounded by a minimum of what seemed to be a hundred police.

The first officer on the scene placed handcuffs on Todd.

"What's your name?"

"I didn't do any fuckin' thing," he responded.

"Sir, what is your name?" the officer repeated.

"Todd Anderson."

"Mr. Anderson, you have the right to remain silent." Just then a shift commander arrived on the scene. "Is that Mr. Anderson?" he asked the officer.

"Yeah, Chief."

"Take those handcuffs off him," he ordered.

An I-told-you-so look appeared on Todd's face when the trooper uncuffed him.

The trooper paid him no mind. He had seen worse looks and had been cursed out enough in similar situations that he had become immune to it.

"Thank you, Chief," Todd said as if the two had known one another their entire life.

Chief Andre Randle had been in law enforcement thirty-three of his fifty-two years of existence, choosing the profession initially thinking he could solve the unsolved murder of his older brother, who was the victim of a racial hate crime one uneventful evening after a bullet took his life while leaving a high school party. He never did crack the case, but had since then solved many others. Being African American and from the Norfolk area gave the chief an advantage over others when it came to the way he did his job. It was, in fact, his street smarts that contributed to his successes over the years. His experience and knowledge of the urban communities earned him a 98 percent crime-solving rate. Today he intended to maintain that number.

"Please come with me, Mr. Anderson," the chief replied.

Todd followed as the police on the scene secured the area. Todd could see flares alongside of the ramp trailing up to the top of the exit, the area being yellow-taped off and officers walking around in search of clues as to what may have happened.

"Mr. Anderson, you were the one who notified nine-one-one, correct?" the chief asked.

"That's correct."

"Can you tell us what you saw?"

"Sure. I was coming down two-sixty-four after leaving my girlfriend Debbie's house out in Virginia Beach, making my way home."

"Where's home?" the officer taking notes asked.

"Right here. Norfolk."

"Okay, go on."

"So, I'm driving down the highway coming up on my exit when I see some asshole, backing his car up off the exit ramp. And I'm thinking to myself, this idiot is lost."

"Why would you think that?" the chief asked.

"Because the car had Washington, D.C. tags on it."

"Did you happen to remember the plate number?" the other officer asked.

"Not really, but the first two letters did stick out," Todd answered.

"Why is that?"

"Because they were our home state's initials."

"You mean *VA*?"

"Yup."

"Okay, that's good. What about the car? Can you tell us the make of the car?"

"Now that I can help you with. That's easy because my aunt Sharon has one just like it, only hers is silver and I think it's a freakin' knockoff of the Magnum and Charger, which I like the Charger best," Todd rambled.

The chief's tolerance was wearing thin. "Mr. Anderson, can you please answer Officer Perez's question?"

"Oh, sorry about that, Chief. Yes, it was a royal blue Dodge Avenger."

"Thank you, Mr. Anderson. Is there anything else you can think of that may be of some help?" the chief asked.

"Uh," he thought. "Oh, I think there were two people in the car and I could be wrong on this one, but it looked like it was a woman driving, an African American woman. That's all I can think of."

"Thank you, Mr. Anderson, you've been more then helpful and I apologize for any inconvenience this may have caused you. Go call it in," he said all in one breath to Todd and the investigating officer.

"On it," the officer hurried.

"You're welcome, Chief. Anytime, just wish I could've been more helpful. I hope you catch the cocksuckin' bastards who did this, though," was Todd's reply.

"So do I," was the chief's response just as he was bombarded with more bad news.

"Chief, we got another one," the officer informed him. "In the back of the armored truck."

Todd stood there, trying to being nosy, hoping to get an earful to add to the story he would tell his friends later in the day.

"Have a good day, Mr. Anderson," the chief dismissed Todd.

Catching the hint, Todd made tracks to his vehicle.

"See to it that Mr. Anderson makes it to his vehicle and safely out of the area," the chief appointed another officer.

The officer knew what the chief had really requested of him. "No problem, chief."

"What do we got?" the chief asked.

"Don't look good, Chief."

"It never does, give it to me."

"Three dead bodies. Two security, the driver forty-eight years old; Gustave Constanza. The passenger; thirty-four years old, Troy Davis, both out of Norfolk. Multiple gunshot wounds to upper and lower parts of the body. We found casings near both bodies, nine millimeters near the driver, nine millimeters and forty calibers near the passenger. In the back of the armored, Thirty-two years old, Judy Smith of Washington D.C., one shot to the head, close range. My guess she was shot somewhere else and placed in the back of the truck."

"That answers where the car came from," the chief said.

"What car, Chief?"

"The one the perps got away in. Witness said he saw a Dodge Avenger with D.C. plates backing off the ramp."

"That explains why we found two motorcycles."

"But why ride motorcycles, then jack a car?" the chief questioned himself, noticing the bikes. "Why not just drive a car? Unless . . ." he answered his own question. "Didn't you say there were two different shell casings near the passenger security guard?"

"Yeah."

"Have someone check his hand and weapon to see whether he fired it or not and have everyone check for traces of blood," the chief ordered as he put the pieces together in his head.

"On it."

Five minutes later the officer returned with the information the chief had already known existed.

"You were right as usual, Chief. It's been confirmed that the security guard's forty caliber was fired. I checked the gun myself. Out of a full clip three bullets were missing. Judging by the way he was laying, chances were he fired at something or rather someone in front of him, so I followed the path and it led me right to a blood trail next to the armored truck," the officer announced, proud of himself for what he believed to be great detective work.

"Good job, Sergeant, have someone run a sample back to headquarters for a DNA immediately."

"Already three steps ahead of you, Chief."

"And also, have them do a printout of anyone in the seven-cities area with bank robbery on their jacket, male and female starting with the city of Norfolk first," the chief requested.

"Gotcha."

The chief placed his hands behind his back and began walking around, scanning the area for something that might leap out at him to help tell the story as to what happened out there. "Come out, come out, wherever you are," he chimed to himself.

Chapter 21

Meanwhile across town, Teflon was just blocks away from her intended destination.

"How you feelin' over there?" she asked Rich.

"As strong as an ox," he answered.

Teflon smiled. His answer was to be expected. "And as smart as a fox." She finished his sentence for him.

"Exactly."

Teflon arrived on the street of the house she had found out social services had assigned little Treach to and parked mere houses away from the address written on the piece of paper. "We're here," she informed Rich.

"Okay, you ready?"

"Most definitely, but you're not. You're in no condition. Just stay here. I'll go in and grab him and be back as soon as I can."

"Like hell," he coughed. "I'm going."

She cut his words short. "Look at you. You're bleeding all over the place, Rich. If you go in with me like that all you're gonna do is leave an easy blood trail for them to follow. It's just a matter of time before they find it back there and run it, so we don't have no time to waste. Trust me, I got this. I'm going to be in and out and I'm not gonna let anything or anyone stand in my way of doing just that. If someone so much as blinks the wrong way I'm gonna cash their ass out. Now let me go in and get your fuckin' grandson so we can get the hell out of VA."

Every word Teflon had said Rich could not argue with. She was 100 percent right. He had already thought about how he had jeopardized their plan by getting caught slipping. He also knew that he was in no condition to get out of the car, let alone make it into the house. Each minute he felt himself getting weaker and weaker. It was his pride that caused him to continue to stand firm, but after hearing Teflon's words he reasoned with himself not to allow his ego to stand in the way of what needed to be done and how it needed to be carried out.

"Hurry up and go get my grandson," he said.

"Thank you."

Teflon checked her guns. She stuck one in the lower part of her back and shoved the other in her shoulder holster.

"Be back in a sec," she assured Rich, leaning over and planting a kiss on his forehead before exiting the Dodge Avenger.

"All right kids, time to do your house chores and freshen up before we eat," the elderly staff lady announced.

Children of all ages ranging from six to sixteen began to scurry to their assigned areas. Most of them had been at the house long enough to incorporate the daily schedule into their daily routine. Treacherous had been at the house for nine months, the longest he had ever been at one place. In total he had been to twenty-three different spots affiliated with social services from the time he was born up until now, none of the others lasting longer than six months. As usual, he kept to himself and only did what he was told, nothing more, nothing less. His job was to take out the trash before and after each meal. Treacherous made his rounds, gathering up the garbage bags that were filled in the cans throughout the house. Retrieving three out of the five bags, he then made his way toward the back of the house. Just as he reached the back door, he heard the front doorbell ring.

Ms. Davis, the head of staff, stopped what she was doing and looked up at the hallway clock on the wall. It was well after visiting hours, she thought as she walked toward the front door to see who was there, wondering who could it be.

She moved the door's curtain to the side. She didn't recognize the woman, but was sure she was one of the children's parents. Maybe one of the new ones, she thought, figuring they were unaware of the visiting schedule.

"Yes, may I help you?" she asked, opening up the front door.

"Yeah, if you don't wanna die," Teflon answered. She had already drawn her gun from behind her back. She pushed her way through the door and aimed her gun to Ms. Davis's face.

Instantly Ms. Davis threw her hands up. "I don't understand," she exclaimed. She had never been so scared in her sixty years of living.

"I came for my son," Teflon announced. Her eyes scanned the house as she spoke. From what she could see all the children and the other staff were preoccupied and her sudden presence had gone unnoticed.

"Young lady, just relax," Ms. Davis tried to reason. In her twenty-five years as a child services worker she had encountered parents who made the same demands but never on such an extreme scale. Nonetheless, she now understood, but there was no way she could have known how serious Teflon actually was or understood the lengths she would go to, though, if she didn't comply with her demand.

"My son's name is Treacherous Freeman. You have two minutes, one to locate him and the other to bring him to me without making a scene, or you will not live to see another day. Are we clear?" Teflon calmly stated.

Between the coldhearted looked she saw in her eyes and her stern tone there was no doubt in Ms. Davis's mind that Teflon meant business.

"Yes," she answered. "Please follow me," she then said.

Teflon concealed her weapon and followed.

"Ms. Davis, I finished straightening up," a little girl bombarded as Teflon and Ms. Davis walked through the house.

"Very good," Ms. Davis's voice cracked. "Now go get ready for super."

The little girl hurried off to do as she was told. Ms. Davis nervously continued to search for Treacherous.

"Is everything okay, Ms. Davis?" one of the male staff members asked, noticing her peculiar facial expression.

"Yes, everything is fine, Tyrone," she carefully replied. She had hoped her voice hadn't cracked like it had when the little girl approached her.

"Okay. Hello," she then addressed Teflon. She nodded her head and shot him an award- winning warm smile. She watched him closely to see if he was aware of any imminent danger. She could tell by the way he was staring at her that something else was on his mind other than her being a threat. Convinced he was clueless, Teflon placed her hand on Ms. Davis's shoulder. "I really need to be going," Teflon hinted.

"Of course," Ms. Davis replied, knowing she was running out of time.

"Tyrone, have you seen Treacherous?"

Tyrone looked at his watch. "He should be out back emptying the trash," he offered.

"That's right," Ms. Davis remembered.

"He should be coming back in now," he added.

"Thank you, Tyrone."

Just then Teflon heard the familiar voice. It took everything in her power not to let the three-letter-word melt her heart.

"Mom?" Treacherous called out. He couldn't believe his eyes when he saw her standing with Ms. Davis and Mr. Waters. Even from the side view, despite only meeting and seeing her once, he could tell it was his mother. It was a face he had locked in and taken to bed with him every night since the first time he had laid eyes on her. Although it was good to see her, Treacherous wondered how she had found him and furthermore, what was she doing there?

"Treach baby, come here," she spoke in a motherly tone.

Ms. Davis remained silent. Treacherous walked over to his mother. Teflon embraced him with her left arm and kissed him on the forehead.

"We're leaving," she told him.

Her words not only surprised Treacherous, but Tyrone as well.

"Ms. Davis, what's going on?" he asked. Teflon could now see in his face that he had figured out something wasn't right. Wasting no time, she sprung into action. Treacherous's eyes widened at the sight of the gun his mother drew.

"Get the fuck over there," she barked, waving the black piece of steel at both Ms. Davis and Tyrone, more so at Tyrone as she placed Treacherous behind her. The bass of her voice echoed throughout the house, alarming the other two female staff on duty and the other thirty-four children it housed.

"Everybody over here," she then commanded, drawing her second weapon.

Fear filled the air as screams and cries of young children outweighed the echo of Teflon's orders.

In seconds everyone in the entire house was packed together in front of Teflon like sardines.

"As long as everyone do as I say nobody will get hurt," Teflon announced.

Children and staff both shook their heads in agreement.

"How many phones are in this house?" she directed her question to Ms. Davis.

"Three," she replied.

"Where?"

"One over on the wall, another at the top of the stairs, and one in my office back there," Ms. Davis made sure to be truthful and accurate.

"Where's your first aid kit?" she then asked.

"It's in my office under my desk."

"Treach, go into the kitchen and get a knife," Teflon instructed her son. "Then go and cut all phone lines, get the first aid kit, and come right back, you hear me?"

"Uh-hm." Treacherous shook his head and hurried to the kitchen.

"Sister, you don't have to do this," Tyrone blurted out.

"Muthafucka I ain't ya sistah now shut the fuck up," Teflon barked.

All the children's eyes widened at Teflon's words.

"Tyrone, please," Ms. Davis begged. The last thing she wanted was for Tyrone to get Teflon riled up.

"What?" He threw his hands up. "I was only trying to help."

Teflon walked over toward him. "You wanna help? Keep your fuckin' mouth shut."

Treacherous was just returning after cutting the last phone line in Ms. Davis's office when he heard his mother screaming on Mr. Waters.

"Anybody with cell phones pull 'em out," she then ordered. The two female staff in the back immediately raised their phones in the air. Ms. Davis did the same in the front, but Tyrone hesitated.

"Treach, go get those." She instructed little Treacherous to retrieve the phones from the back.

Tyrone couldn't believe Teflon was up in his face the way she was. The fact that she had a gun pointed at him meant nothing to him. Ever since she had first drawn the weapons he was tempted to try her, but instead he took a different route, a route Teflon had no way of knowing. Tyrone was not at all threatened or intimidated by her. He had grown up in the streets of Virginia and had been around guns all of his life and had actually carried one himself at some point, and she didn't seem like she knew how to handle one. Tyrone perceived her as a typical enraged mother who had gone to the extreme to reunite with her son. He was convinced in his mind that he could still talk her down before she made a huge mistake. He had no way of knowing that his analogy was way off.

"Think about what you're doing." Rather than complying with Teflon's demand he made another attempt to reason with her. "It's not too late."

"Yes it is," she calmly said just as the bullet exited the chamber of her gun and entered Tyrone Waters's mouth.

The shot caused Ms. Davis to faint and one of the female staff to vomit while all the kids and the other female staff now screamed uncontrollably.

"Everybody be quiet and no one else will be hurt," Teflon assured them all.

She knew it was time to get out of the group home. She stepped over Tyrone's body and retrieved Ms. Davis's cellular phone, which had hit the ground right before she had. She then turned back to Tyrone's lifeless body and snatched his phone out of his hip clip. When she grabbed his phone Teflon could hear a voice coming from it. She looked at the screen of Tyrone Waters's phone.

"Fuck," she exclaimed, seeing the number 911 plastered across the screen. The call showed that it had been running for the past three minutes. Teflon cursed herself for not noticing Tyrone dialing the number.

"Treacherous baby, let's get up outta here," she told her son.

Treacherous made his way over to Teflon. Before she made her way to the front door Teflon pumped two more bullets into Tyrone's lifeless body, then tucked one of her guns, grabbed Treacherous's arm, and scurried to the door. Everyone jumped at the sounds of the shots. One of the female staff rushed to Ms. Davis as soon as she heard the front door slam.

Chapter 22

Chief Randle was just making his way back toward the armored truck when he heard his name called. He could see excitement in his sergeant's face as he approached him. "Tell me something to make me smile," he told the sergeant.

"How about this," the sergeant began. "We got a positive ID on the DNA we found. You ready?" the sergeant asked.

"I'm listening."

"DNA belongs to a Mr. Richard Robinson."

"Robinson?" The chief ran the name around his head.

"Come on, Chief, I was told you would recognize the name."

"Richard Robinson?" he continued to ponder.

"Maybe this will refresh your memory. I did like you said and had them pull up all ex-cons who had any type of armed robbery on their jacket, male and female, starting with the ones in the local area from the biggest to the smallest and guess what?"

"Come with it," the chief welcomed.

"Richard Robinson's name was number two on the list. He served over twenty-five years for armed robbery. Got caught after he got away with over a million dollars from Bank of America. Ring any bells?"

The moment the sergeant made mention of the bank's name and how long ago the case was the bells began to burst his eardrums. He now knew why the name Richard Robinson had stood out to him. It was his first time working a bank job as a detective. It was also the case that had gotten him promoted to head detective in his division.

"You gots to be kiddin' me. I thought he was dead," the chief chimed.

"Nope, alive and kicking. But wait, it gets better," the sergeant continued.

"Do you remember about ten years ago the same bank was hit again by a young couple?"

"Now that I remember," the chief answered. "It was all over the news when I came back from vacation. I was pissed I wasn't here to work the case. I think they were calling them the modern-day Bonnie and Clyde. The goddamn boyfriend battled it out not too far from here on two-sixty-four, if I remember and the girlfriend was found unconscious in the car."

"You remember right," the sergeant said. "But there's something you forgot about that whole incident."

"What's that?" the chief was eager to know.

"That the boyfriend was Richard Robinson's son."

"Jesus, how could I forget," the chief retorted.

"Wait, though. When the list for the females came out, guess whose name popped up?"

The chief didn't have to guess that one. "The girlfriend."

"The girlfriend," the sergeant repeated. "Seems her federal sentence was overturned and she's been out for a few months now. May be a long shot, but . . ."

The chief and sergeant were interrupted by one of the officers on the scene.

"Excuse me, Chief, dispatcher thought you might be interested in a nine-one-one call that just came in. They think it may be connected to the armored truck hit." He handed the chief the walkie-talkie.

"This is Chief Randle, go."

"Hey Chief, this is Wendy. Nine-one-one forwarded me this call that came in about five minutes ago. You listening?"

"Yeah Wendy, let me hear it."

"Sister, you don't have to do this."

"Muthafucka I aint' ya sistah now shut the fuck up."

"Tyrone, please."

"What? I was only trying to help."

"You wanna help? Keep your fuckin' mouth shut."

"Anybody with cell phones pull 'em out."

"Treach, go get those."

"Think about what you're doing. It's not too late."

"Yes it is."

"Christ," Chief Randle bellowed, hearing the shot go off. He didn't have to witness it to know the female perp had just killed the man talking. Screams of children could be heard in the background.

"Everybody be quiet and no one else will be hurt."

"Fuck. Treacherous baby, let's get up outta here."

The tape ended. "That's all we got, Chief, think it's connected."

Chief was already putting it together in his mind.

"Wendy, do me a favor, play the ending back one more time for me," he requested as something leaped out at him. He wanted to be sure he had heard what he'd thought he had.

"Sure."

"Everybody be quiet and no one else will be hurt."

"Fuck. Treacherous baby, let's get up outta here."

"Son of a bitch."

This time the sergeant caught it as well.

"Chief, are you thinking what I'm thinking?"

"I am, but it's impossible. There's no way Treacherous Freeman could still be alive. Hell, the shit was on national television, un- less . . ." the chief said in mid-sentence.

"Wendy get me an address on that location ASAP."

"Already have it."

"Unless what, Chief?" The sergeant couldn't figure it out.

"Those were kids screaming in the back- ground, right?"

"Yeah, so?" The sergeant was still in the dark.

"So maybe Treacherous was a kid."

"Her son?"

"Exactly."

As soon as he said it the dispatcher came back on the line. "Chief, the address is to a group home for kids. You ready?"

"Shoot," he said as the smirk appeared on his face. Once he jotted the address down, Chief Randle made a mad dash for his vehicle.

Chapter 23

Rich opened his eyes at the sound of the car door opening. He smiled when he saw Teflon getting in the front seat and little Treacherous in the back. Teflon looked over at Rich to check on him.

"You good?"

He nodded his head.

"Treach, hand me that box."

Treacherous handed his mother the first aid kit. "We need to put something on your neck right quick." Teflon opened the box and pulled out the peroxide, gauze pads, and a cloth roll. She leaned into Rich. "This may sting a bit, man up."

Rich smiled. He braced himself and clinched his teeth as the sensation of the over-the-counter liquid ignited his insides. Treacherous watched from the back as his mother nursed the stranger's wound.

"Hold this," she instructed Rich, placing his hand on the gauze pads. Quickly she wrapped the cloth roll around his neck. Under the circumstances she knew she had done the best she could. Once she felt she had Rich's wound sedated, Teflon started the car and peeled off. The peroxide and bandages Teflon dressed his neck wound with brought a little relief to Rich's discomfort.

Rich managed to shift his body and looked back at his grandson. He couldn't believe the strong resemblance of his son when Treacherous was his age. "Hey li'l man," he spoke in a low, raspy tone.

Treacherous did not answer, though. He wondered who the man was that sat in the front passenger seat. Whoever he was Treacherous could see that he was bleeding. Rich's blood had soiled the side of the passenger seat.

"Say hello to your grandfather," Teflon told him.

"Hi," Treacherous kept it short.

"That's your father's dad," she explained.

Rich grinned. Treacherous noticed the grin resembled the same one he often found himself displaying at times for different reasons.

"We have plenty of time to get to know each other," Rich said to Treacherous before turning back around.

"So what took so long?" Rich asked.

"Tsk, it got crazy in there. Some muthafucka tried to play Dr. Phil and I had to slump his dumb ass."

"So much for in-and-out smooth. No kids, right?"

"No kids, but this piece of shit I was tellin' you about snuck and called nine-one-one. Don't really know all they got, but his phone was on for about three minutes."

Rich frowned. Hearing that he knew it was just a matter of time before authorities got on their trail if they hadn't already.

"We gotta get out of VA right now," Rich managed to say through coughs.

"I know," Teflon agreed as she accelerated on the pedal.

Chapter 24

Chief Randle was just minutes away from the group home when the unexpected call came through.

"Chief Randle, are you there?"

"This is Chief Randle, go."

"Just got a call saying they got a visual on that royal blue Dodge Avenger. It's heading northbound on two-sixty-four near Interstate sixty-four. They're redirecting out all available units."

The news caused the chief to slam on brakes. He threw the patrol car in reverse, backed up to the intersection's opening he had just passed, and made a U-turn in the middle of the highway after traveling southbound. The chief wasted no time darting out into the ongoing traffic. He floored the gas pedal until the speedometer read 120.

Fifteen miles up the highway Teflon contin-ued to gaze up at the helicopter that seemed to surface every five minutes as she navigated the Dodge. She couldn't help but think about the last time a helicopter hovered over her on a highway, but shook the thought off.

"I keep seein' that damn helicopter," she pointed to Rich.

"Yeah me too," Rich said. He was convinced they were being followed. He had enough run-ins to know when the heat was on. He could practically feel them breathing down their necks.

"I think I should get off and switch cars," Teflon suggested.

Rich shook his head in disagreement. "If they're on us that'll be a bad move. As soon as we get off they'll be swarming us."

"If we stay in this it's gonna be the same thing. We can't outrun anything in this slow-ass muthafucka."

Rich was thinking the same thing, but knew they had no time to make any type of pit stops. He looked up and saw that the copter was still in view of them.

"We can't stop," Rich stated.

Teflon sighed and looked back at her son. "You okay, man?"

"Um-hm." Treacherous shook his head. He sat quietly and listened to his mother and grandfather's conversation. Little by little he was putting the pieces together as best his young mind would allow him. Although he was glad to be with his mother, he still couldn't figure why she had come to get him the way she had. Whatever the case, he knew it wasn't good. Then just like that, the worst appeared.

Teflon saw the state trooper patrol car alongside the road to her left. A bad feeling began to invade her.

"Just be cool," Rich said.

"I'm cool."

They both were aware of the fact that troopers posted up all throughout the interstate and had hoped that was the case, but as she passed the patrol car their hopes became a distant thought that vanished into thin air.

"Damn," she cursed.

The flashing lights of the state trooper's patrol car appeared in the rearview mirror of the Avenger.

Rich strained to reach down on the floor in front of him.

"Baby, put your seat belt on," Telfon instructed Treacherous. She looked over to see Rich preparing what they both knew was to come.

Rich checked his AR-15 then sat it in his lap.

"Treach, reach under Mommy's seat and pass that up to me."

Treacherous unfastened his seat belt, reached under the driver's seat, retrieved the identical replica of the weapon Rich had, and handed it to his mother. Treacherous noticed a vanilla-colored envelope under his mother's seat as well.

Teflon placed her AR-15 between her and Rich.

"Thank you, man, now put your seat belt back on."

Treacherous did what he was told.

"You want me to stop?"

"Might as well," Rich replied. "We're all in now. Ride or die, right?"

"Ride or die."

The trooper had already unsnapped the latch of his gun holster and drew his weapon as he stepped out of his patrol car. He cautiously made his way over to the passenger side of the vehicle. Despite the report saying the suspects were armed and dangerous, he decided against waiting for backup and instead approached the vehicle with his weapon pointed at the front-seat occupants.

"Ma'am, turn off the vehicle and let me see your hands, both of you" he shouted, his eyes going back and forth from Teflon to Rich. Seeing that no one complied the trooper became more aggressive with his tone. "Ma'am, turn the vehicle off now!" Had he focused more on Rich he may have seen it coming before he felt it.

Rich let off a barrage of shots through the back windshield, six of the eight shots cutting the trooper down where he stood. Teflon snatched the gearshift into drive and jumped back onto the highway.

"Treach, are you okay, baby?" she asked with motherly concern. She had told him to get on the floor and cover his head, knowing what Rich intended to do.

"Yes," he answered. Treacherous could feel the glass debris hitting his back as his grandfather launched his assault on the trooper. The shots rang off in his ears like fireworks on the Fourth of July, thought Treacherous. For the first time since his mother had taken him from the group home young Treacherous was afraid.

"I'm sorry," he heard his grandfather say to his mother.

Rich was not a man of many regrets, but seeing how what he thought to be a foolproof plan beginning to unfold he began to regret ever proposing all they had done hours ago to Teflon.

"I told you about talkin' crazy," Teflon replied. "You didn't put a gun to my head or in my hand.

I signed up for this shit, remember. We in this together."

Her response was not surprising to Rich.

"Look," she said, pointing.

"It ends here," Rich retorted, seeing the two state trooper cars zooming onto the interstate.

"Treacherous, stay down," she told her son.

He could tell by her tone another problem had occurred. All that had happened so far seemed surreal to Treacherous. It was like watching a 3-D movie, he told himself, only with real guns, real people, and real blood.

"We got more company." Rich was the one who pointed this time. Three more cars traveling southbound looped around through the grass that divided the interstate.

By now Teflon had the speedometer to the max. Switching lanes and blowing the horn like a madwoman, Teflon wished Treacherous was there with her.

Her thoughts were interrupted by the sounds of a beep. The gas light appeared on the dashboard as the needle rested on the letter E. Teflon and Rich exchanged looks without uttering a word. Their silence spoke volumes.

Chapter 25

Chief Randle saw the state trooper car up ahead alongside of the shoulder of the interstate and assumed it was the one that had called in the stop. When he didn't see the Avenger alongside the highway also he automatically thought the worse. His thoughts were confirmed as he got close up on the car.

"Fuck," he cursed, seeing the trooper's body laying alongside the road.

He immediately picked up the walkie-talkie, radioed it in, and floored the gas pedal.

Within minutes Chief Randle could see the convoy of police cars up ahead. Traffic continued to pull to each side to allow him to pass as his silent siren's light flashed on top of his patrol car. The more the highway parted like the Red Sea the quicker Chief Randle caught up to the other police cars, passing some along the way.

In no time he could see the back of the royal blue Dodge Avenger. He could see the Dodge weaving in and out of the traffic up ahead. Seeing the way the car maneuvered caused Chief Randle to reflect back on the time he had witnessed the last high-speed chase on WAVY 10 news on this very same highway with the girl and Richard Robinson's son. He wondered what could possibly be going through the minds of the duo he and his colleagues were in pursuit of. His thought came to an end when it looked as if the Dodge Avenger was stopping.

"This is it," Teflon turned to Rich as the Dodge began to jerk.

She knew they were just mere feet away from being trialed, convicted, and sentenced. Just as before when she had found herself in a similar predicament with her other half, although she didn't intend for it to end this way, she was prepared for the final fate she and Rich had chosen for themselves. All she could think about was leaving her only child with nothing or no one to love, take care of, and watch over him. Tears of anger began to trickle down her face at the thought.

"Treach, promise me that no matter what, whatever happens, you'll stay down," she stated as the car drove its last mile.

"Okay," he replied from the back.

"Promise me."

"I promise." he quickly responded.

"That's my man."

She then directed her attention back to Rich. He appeared to have regained some strength from somewhere, she thought, seeing the familiar look in his eyes. It was the look of a bona fide gangster.

"You ready?" he asked.

"Born ready," she replied. There was a long pause. Something had been weighing heavy on Rich's mind and heart and he was undecided on whether he should share with Teflon or not since he had taken the shots back at the armored truck and even before then. Teflon could see by the expression on his face there was something wrong. It was the same expression that appeared on his son's when he was fighting with his thoughts or feelings toward something.

"What's wrong?" She broke the silence.

The question helped Rich make up his mind. "Nothing's wrong," he started out saying. "There's just something I wanted to tell you. Something I wanted you to know. I didn't want it to end like this without you knowing."

"Knowing what?" Teflon became impatient seeing that Rich was beating around the bush about something. "Why you talkin' in riddles?" Teflon questioned as their two eyes locked.

Rich let out a half of a chuckle holding Teflon's stare. He felt like a kid in high school all over again. As hard core and as gangster of an individual he felt himself to be he couldn't believe how nervous he was. He was more nervous saying what he was about to say than he was about what was about to happen to them on the highway. Rather than prolong it any longer he decided to come out and say it.

"I just wanted you to know that I am in love with—"

The word *you* was silenced by the bullet that penetrated the back of Rich's head. He had never got to tell Teflon how he had been secretly in love with her since the first day she had come home from prison. Rich's head landed on Teflon's shoulder. The shot the sharpshooter delivered was responsible for the blood that temporarily dyed her face.

"Nooooo!" she yelled as she attempted to lift him up. "Rich!" You could hear the pain in her cries as Teflon screamed frantically.

The second shot shattered the driver's-side window, barely missing her head.

"Ma?" Treacherous rose up and yelled. He had no way of knowing the shots that were to follow ended because of him.

Chapter 26

"Seize fire!" the chief exclaimed. "I repeat, seize fire. This is Chief Randle, there is a child—abort," he shouted into the walkie-talkie.

From where Chief Randle stood positioned behind his patrol car he was the only senior officer on the scene who had seen the little boy's head surface. He knew the kid was none other than Teflon Jackson's son. The last thing he wanted to see was for a child to get caught in the crossfire or worse, witness his mother get gunned down right before his very eyes.

"Copy that," the sharpshooter replied. He too now saw the kid in the backseat.

Chief Randle made his way over to the closest officer. "Who's in charge?" he asked, approaching.

"Lieutenant Lyles." An officer pointed two cars up to the left.

Chief Randle kept his head low and made his way over to the superior officer on the scene.

Hearing that he outranked the officer despite being out of his jurisdiction made him feel more confident with his decision.

"Lieutenant Lyles?" he asked, seeing the gold bar on the lieutenant's shirt.

"What can I do for you?" the lieutenant answered, not bothering to turn around. His focus was on the car ahead.

"I'm Chief Randle. I heard you were in charge here."

"You heard right," the lieutenant replied, now turning around.

"Well, these particular perps are connected to an armored truck case up two-sixty-four I'm heading. Perps' names are Richard Robinson and Teflon Jackson, both convicted felons, armed-robbery charges, both bank jobs."

"Chief, with all due respect I appreciate you having my man stand down due to a child being in the vehicle, but this is my scene and we got it from here," he said as his eyes shifted back and forth from the chief to the Dodge Avenger.

"I'm not trying to take over here, I'm just lending a helping hand. Correct me if I'm wrong, but at the end of the day we do want the best outcome with minimum incident as possible," Chief Randle expressed.

Lt. Lyles studied Chief Randle for a few seconds. "Absolutely, Chief," the lieutenant then replied. "What do you know?"

Chief Randle began to brief the lieutenant on everything he knew about Teflon, Rich, and the case.

Chapter 27

"Treacherous are you hurt?" Teflon asked as she reclined the seat of the Avenger.

"No." The sound of her son's voice snapped her out of the semi-trance she had just been in. The shot that had ended Rich's life had come out of nowhere and all she could think about were his last words before he breathed his last breath. She played them back over and over in her head. She thought she'd heard him wrong, but knew she hadn't. She knew now was not the time or place for her to be dwelling on Rich's words or death, but she couldn't help but think about how he could have felt the way he had about her. She was positive that she hadn't done anything intentional to fuel his feelings, but at the same time understood. Teflon shook off his words, but couldn't shake Rich's death. Although they had prepared themselves for the worst, she did not expect Rich's sudden demise. Her thoughts were moving at a lightning-speed pace.

She knew her own time was nearing and coming to an end and was ready to embrace it, but she couldn't stop thinking about where that would leave her son. Returning back to prison was not an option for Teflon. She told herself when she had come home that she would rather be carried by six then to be condemned by twelve. For her prison was the most degrading and worst time of her life. She felt prison was contributing to her animalistic way of thinking and behavior and that's exactly what she had felt like: a caged animal. Being someone who had always had a problem with authority and taking orders from another she found no pleasure in being told when to eat, sleep, shower, or any other luxuries one should have the right to do as they please. The more she thought about it the more she realized that would be the type of life she'd be leaving her son to be subjected to and that upset her. Teflon reasoned with herself that with his bloodline her son was destined to travel down the same paths that she and his father had and she did not want to take that chance. Just as she made her final decision she heard the voice boom through the bullhorn.

Chief Randle was grateful that Lt. Lyles had allowed him to take control over the situation.

They knew it was just a matter of time before the feds arrived on the scene and the both of them lost all control over the matter. Coming to an agreement for him to take charge, Chief Randle grabbed the bullhorn.

"Ms. Jackson, this is Chief Randle of the Norfolk police department. As you can see we have you surrounded. No one else has to get hurt," he tried to reason. "It doesn't have to end this way. I give you my word if you place your weapons outside of the vehicle and exit the car slowly nothing will happen to you. If not for you, please consider your child," the chief added, appealing to her maternal side. Remembering the last time she found herself in the similar predicament, Chief Randle knew Teflon Jackson had no problem ending things in the middle of the highway. To his surprise, the driver's door flung open.

"Hold your fire," the chief ordered.

Teflon couldn't help but laugh. *Same shit, different day*, she thought, reflecting back to the similar words the negotiating officer had offered her and Treacherous the last time she found herself in the similar predicament. She wondered had Treacherous felt the way she was feeling at that very moment. She reached her hand up and brushed it gently across Rich's face.

"Come here, man," she then said to Treacherous. "Climb over here."

A confused Treacherous did as his mother requested. Teflon noticed the vanilla envelope in her son's hand that she had under the seat. She had actually forgotten she had placed the book she had written about her and his father underneath the driver's seat. Seeing the envelope now made Teflon wonder who would pick up where she had left off and finish the story, because she knew her final chapter had arrived. With that being her thought, Teflon grabbed hold of the car handle and pushed the door open.

Chapter 28

The first thing Chief Randle saw was the assault rifle hit the pavement when the door of the Dodge opened. The lieutenant was impressed at the rapid progress the chief had displayed. He had actually anticipated a more tragic ending on the interstate due to the circumstances and history the chief had given him on the suspects. He hadn't been involved in many standoffs or negotiations, but the few he did had never ended nicely. He watched closely as a leg appeared out of the car.

"I can't believe it Chief, you did it," the lieutenant congratulated.

"Not yet," Chief Randle calmly replied. "Everyone hold your fire," he ordered for a second time. He was fully aware of how riled up officers could get when one of their own had been shot or slain and knew all officers on the scene were antsy and itching for one false move on the suspect's part.

Chief Randle watched steadily as Teflon Jackson rose up. He could see a portion of her body appear out of the vehicle. As she carefully made an attempt to climb out of the car the chief noticed the additional legs that dangled in front of her.

Teflon reached over and grabbed hold of the AR-15. She tossed it out of the car so that the authorities could see that she was surrendering.

"You gotta trust Mommy on this okay, baby," Teflon said to her son as she rose up.

"Okay."

"Good, now hold Mommy tight." She half smiled and kissed him on the side of the face.

Treacherous wrapped his arms around his mother's neck and squeezed tightly.

She reached for her Glock 40 and began exiting the vehicle.

Just as she climbed out the car fully Treacherous could feel the cold steel pressed against his temple.

"Go ahead and shoot me muthafucka," Teflon shouted, now out of the car, walking in the direction of the dozens of police.

"Stand down," Chief Randle roared into the bullhorn. He along with everyone else saw the gun Teflon held up against the child's head.

"No, shoot," she spit back, continuing to approach them.

"Ma, what are you doing?" a scared Treacherous asked. It was the first time he had actually questioned his mother on anything since they had been together.

"Shut up," was the only response he got.

"Ms. Jackson please, don't do this. Don't do this to your child," Chief Randle continued with his persuasion.

Based on the circumstances he didn't know how much longer he could keep his fellow officers at bay.

"You don't know me. You don't know shit about me or mine," she retorted, pressing the gun even harder against her son's head.

"Okay, you're right," he said apologetically. "I don't know you or anything about you, but I know that right now you don't care about dying," the chief added, speaking the obvious. "But what about your son? Don't you care about his life?"

Chief Randle's last words caused Teflon to break out into an insane laughter.

She knew he had no idea as to where her head was at that point.

"What about my son? Do I care about his life," she repeated his question with a chuckle.

A bad feeling swept through the chief's body at the sound of her words. Not what she had said, but how she had said them. Where he was once subtle, the chief was now in full-alert mode.

Tears began to wail up in Teflon's eyes as she fought them off. "Son," she started out. "I want you to know that I did this because I love you. I'll see you daddy and grandpa when I get there," Teflon said all in one breath before she began to apply pressure to the trigger of her Glock 40- cal.

"Hold your fire!" Chief Randle ordered with a wave of his hand as he rushed the two bodies that had hit the pavement with his weapon still drawn. The lieutenant and other officers on the scene trailed behind him. Everything happened so fast no one even knew where the shot had come from.

Chief Randle shook his head in disappointment as he reached the bodies lying on the ground. This was not the way he intended for things to end, but knew it was a possibility.

"Are you okay?" he asked, kneeling next to the bodies.

Treacherous did not reply. He was still in shock.

Chief Randle grimaced at the sight of Teflon sprawled out on the pavement with eyes wide open. He had no other choice, he reasoned.

His options were limited, he told himself as he saw the hole from the shot he fired between her eyes. Either he shot her or he allowed her to shoot her son and he couldn't let that happen. In the end a life was taken so that one could be spared, the chief chalked it up as. He felt for the young boy.

"I'm sorry, kid," he offered. "Didn't mean for it to go down like this."

Still Treacherous said nothing. He continued to lay his head rested on his mother's chest. He didn't have to look up and see the bullet hole between her eyes to know she was dead. He could not hear her heartbeat or feel her breathing. He wept for the loss of his mother as silent tears soiled her shirt.

Chief Randle rose. He understood the silence from the boy and knew there wasn't anything he could do to console him. Before he knew it every officer and medical team was on the scene. "Can one of you get the boy," he stated more then asked, directing his words to one of the EMTs.

The EMT rushed over, kneeled down, and scooped Treacherous up.

"Come on, young fella."

Surprisingly to the chief, Treacherous did not resist. He had expected him to throw a tantrum, but he continued to remain silent.

"I don't think he's hurt, but check him out anyway, he may be in shock," Chief Randle instructed just as they had reached the ambulance.

"Sure thing, Chief."

"Take it easy," the chief then said to Treacherous.

His words caused Treacherous to turn and face him. The chief was taken aback by the look that appeared on Treacherous's face. "You killed my mother," Treacherous let out. "I won't ever forget you." His words were cold and murderous.

The EMT's eyes widened, but the chief remained calm. The young boy's words were to be expected after all he had just been through and witnessed, thought the chief. He did an about-face and began walking off.

"Chief?" the EMT called out.

When Chief Randle turned around he saw the EMT holding up a vanilla envelope.

"What do you want me to do with this? The kid had it."

"What's in it?"

The EMT skimmed through the contents of the envelope. "Just some papers, it looks like letters."

"Let him keep it," the chief replied. He figured they were letters written by the boy's mother to him.

He turned back around and started making his way back over to the car. He walked right up on the coroner covering the body of Teflon Jackson.

What a tragic day, Chief Randle thought as he peered into the Dodge Avenger.

Epilogue

Two months later

"Treacherous, it's time to eat," the elderly woman called up to the top of the steps.

Since they had placed him into a new group home in Richmond, Treacherous had isolated and alienated himself from everyone in the facility as much as he could. For the past couple of months all he did was stay in his room and read. The only times he in fact left his room were to eat, shower, or use the bathroom; then he was back to his bed. In a short period of time he had learned a great deal about his parents through the pages his mother had written. Her death was still fresh in Treacherous's mind and the incident that lead to her demise began to make sense to him each time he completed a chapter of the story. It became apparent to him that he came from a bloodline of gangsters. It made him feel good to know that his parents loved one another and that he wasn't just the result of a mistake and was intentionally abandoned. He read in amazement at the type of man and woman his father and mother were. That explained the anger he had built up inside of himself, he realized. The same anger he now harbored for the man named Chief Randle who had killed his mother. That day Treacherous locked the man's face in responsible for his mother's death. He vowed to himself that the two would cross paths again and when they did it would be on his terms.

"Treacherous, we're all waiting on you, dear," the elderly woman called out for a second time.

Treacherous sighed out of irritation. He wanted to finish up the chapter he had just been reading before he went down to eat. He hurried to read the last few sentences that would bring the chapter to an end before he closed the notebook.

Treacherous walked over to where each body lay and lodged another shot into them.

"Let's get the hell up outta here," Pete suggested, snatching up the bag with the drugs and money once Treacherous had reached the final body.

"Nah, you stayin'" Treacherous said to Pete right before he pumped three rounds into his face.

Even I did not expect that, but was not surprised. I knew my man had good reason. Without me having to ask he said, "I didn't like the way the nigga tried to challenge me in front of you at the rest stop."

I had a feeling that was the case because Pete's words didn't sit right with me either when he told Treacherous he would remember that he gave him an invitation for a rematch.

Like always, Treacherous and I made it out in one piece and back to our bikes. We gathered up our belongings, wiped down the motel room, and cut our Memorial week short.

Young Treacherous closed the notepad and slipped it under his mattress. As always, he felt a sense of belonging each time he finished reading. Seeing that he was nearly coming to an end of the pages in the second notebook, Treacherous had already made up his mind that he would continue writing where his mother had left off, telling his version of her last days and couldn't wait until the day where he'd be old enough to pick up where his family had left off, hoping one day he would find the type of woman his father had in his mother to be his ride or die chick!